Praise for Beth Williamson's *Hell For Leather*

Rating: 5 Cups "...an exciting story laced with humor. I loved the dark, broody Cade."

~ *Coffee Time Romance*

Rating: 5 Hearts "Once again, Ms. Williamson has penned a book I found almost impossible to put down...a magnificent work of art..."

~ *The Romance Studio*

"Not a typical Western tale, HELL FOR LEATHER is a story about redemption and self-forgiveness...a fascinating story."

~ *Romance Reviews Today*

"No one writes western erotic romance like Beth Williamson. She combines tough and gritty heroes with strong and feisty heroines and the results are fabulous. Hell for Leather is such a novel."

~ *Joyfully Reviewed*

Look for these titles by
Beth Williamson

Now Available:
The Malloy Family Series
The Bounty (Book 1)
The Prize (Book 2)
The Reward (Book 3)
The Treasure (Book 4)
The Gift (Book 5)
The Tribute (Book 6)
The Legacy (Book 7)

The Devils on Horseback Series
Devils on Horseback: Nate (Book 1)
Devils on Horseback: Jake (Book 2)
Devils on Horseback: Zeke (Book 3)

Marielle's Marshal
Branded

Print Anthologies
Midsummer Night's Steam: Sand, Sun and Sex
Leather and Lace

Hell For Leather

Beth Williamson

A SAMHAIN PUBLISHING, LTD. publication.

Samhain Publishing, Ltd.
577 Mulberry Street, Suite 1520
Macon, GA 31201
www.samhainpublishing.com

Hell For Leather
Copyright © 2009 by Beth Williamson
Print ISBN: 978-1-60504-165-0
Digital ISBN: 978-1-60504-046-2

Editing by Sasha Knight
Cover by Scott Carpenter

First Samhain Publishing, Ltd. electronic publication: June 2008
First Samhain Publishing, Ltd. print publication: April 2009

Dedication

To everyone who has ever thought themselves beyond saving, beyond redemption, beyond the reach of love, may you find the light, the peace and the happiness you richly deserve.

Prologue

The cheap whiskey burned as it slid down Kincaid's throat like an old friend. A man not used to such rotgut would've choked. The smells and sounds of the saloon were a buzz in the back of his mind, but he didn't really notice them much.

It was the girl.

The same blonde he'd seen a year ago singing up on stage like a songbird was now serving drinks, looking like a used-up washrag. She'd been bright-eyed and sweet, no more than sixteen, and now she looked haggard, could pass for thirty. He'd seen it happen so many times. He shouldn't be even thinking about her or her fate, but he was.

He blamed it on the damn Malloys. If he hadn't gotten caught up in their lives, he would be as numb as he had been most of his life.

Kincaid slung back the rest of the amber liquid then stood. He told himself to walk out of the saloon, but somehow his feet found their way to the little blonde. As he pressed a golden eagle into her palm, he whispered in her ear.

"Get out of here as fast as you can."

She looked startled, but she didn't pull away, proving she had a backbone. Good, she'd need one to escape from a life in hell.

"Who are you, mister?"

"I'm nobody. A dead man come to life to tell you to get your ass out of here."

With that, he walked out into the bright Wyoming sunlight. His act of kindness surprised even him. Maybe she'd get out in time to save her life, or may he'd just given her enough money to prolong it an extra six months. Didn't matter because he wasn't going to be around to find out.

It was time to bury Kincaid and bring Cade Brody to life.

Chapter One

November 1889

The sun burned off the morning frost, giving rise to mists all along the mossy forest floor. Shafts of light followed his footsteps as Cade Brody walked along with his burlap sack and shovel. He continued on until he found an enormous pine tree with a huge broken branch jutting out from the middle. Although he planned on never being near this damn tree again, he had to know how to find it, just in case.

He set the sack down and used the shovel to clear away the pine needles and leaves. His breath came out in white puffs, letting him know the foothills of the Sangre de Cristo Mountains felt the bite of the cold weather to come. He dug until he'd made a narrow hole three feet in depth. Should be enough to keep any critters or humans out of his business.

Cade set the shovel aside and squatted down on his haunches. When he gripped the rough fabric of the sack, he cursed to see his hand shaking. It wasn't that hard to bury yourself, but damned if he didn't feel a bit sick as he lowered his former life into the ground. He'd made the decision two months ago to kill himself and now he was taking the final step.

He closed his eyes and thought about everything he was leaving behind, a whole lot of nothing, and opened his eyes to see what he was gaining. In the spring, his little valley would be beautiful. Now it was a dying land with an echo of life in its colorful leaves.

Cade finally let go of the bag, and it tumbled into the hole. He stared down into the darkness, wondering if he'd made the right choice, knowing it was almost too late to go back. Almost, but not quite, because he could simply pick up the sack and leave New Mexico.

He stood and wiped his hands on the brown trousers he'd gotten from a friend. No longer the silky black he'd become accustomed to, his new clothes reflected his new life—simple. It was time to accept it and move on.

The first shovelful of dirt was the hardest, but after that, he filled the hole without stopping. He spread the dirt displaced by the sack on the ground around the hole, then covered everything again with pine needles and leaves. Cade stared at the blister on his hand and imagined the calluses he'd have this time next year. This was just the beginning of many to come.

He glanced around and found a piece of white quartz to mark the spot. With a little bit of digging, he wiggled the rock into place. It wasn't much of a grave marker, but it'd do.

Cade stood and pulled off his hat, pressing it to his chest.

"Dear Lord, keep this man safe from harm and take him into your kingdom. He ain't worth more than spit in the wind, but he's yours now. Amen."

With that, Cade Brody picked up his shovel and walked back to his horse, certain he'd buried Kincaid for good. It was time to become the new man he'd chosen to be.

The cabin was in surprisingly good shape. The lawyer in Santa Fe said the previous owner had died six months earlier and no one had claimed it. Cade had been the lucky person who had made an offer to purchase it. The county had been all too willing to unload a property out in the middle of nowhere at the base of the mountains.

About time the damn blood money paid for something other than whiskey, whores or food. As he approached the cabin, a strange feeling crept through him. The cabin wasn't anything special as far as houses go, in fact a layer of dirt and pine needles peppered the outside.

Cade didn't feel as though it was home, only a house. After all, there wasn't anyone waiting for him, just an empty building—except for a critter or two. Yet, that strange feeling remained. Damned if he could figure it out though.

The door opened easily, which was a surprise. He reached for the gun that didn't rest on his hip anymore.

"Shit."

With a frown that could likely scare small children, he stepped into the cabin in a crouch. A quick look around revealed only one room in the cabin, and aside from a chair and a bare mattress frame, there was nothing and no one there.

The nothing concerned him more than the no one. There was no dirt, no twigs, no raccoon shit, just *nothing* in the cabin. Someone had been keeping it clean and it wasn't Cade. The fireplace showed fresh ashes. They were cold so it had been at least a few days, but someone had been there.

This wasn't exactly what he wanted to see or deal with. Jesus Christ, the cabin was *his*, not some squatter's. No doubt he'd have to scare the idiot off too. A scrape against the outside wall had him running to find whoever or whatever had made the noise. A thrill raced through him as he burst out the door and ran around to the back of the cabin. He nearly tripped over a wooden bucket, but saved himself by slamming his left hand into the side of the cabin.

A dozen splinters later, he got his balance back and made it to the tree line figuring whoever it was would've run for cover. Thank God he'd worked his ass off on Malloy's ranch back in Wyoming or he'd have been breathing like a locomotive. Two minutes later, he realized he was chasing air. Nothing marked the ground or brush around him except his own passage.

Cade put his hands on his hips and closed his eyes, straining to hear the sounds of the forest. Except for his heartbeat, he heard nothing out of the ordinary, not a whisper of someone who didn't belong.

He talked to the trees, hoping his trespasser was within shouting distance. "Whoever you are, the cabin belongs to me now. If you come back, you and me are going to have a problem. Go squat someplace else."

He stood there for five minutes, scanning the woods around him. With another muttered curse, he headed back to the cabin alone, pulling out the splinters as he went. By the time he reached the bucket, he'd gotten most of them out. When he glanced down, he stopped short and picked up the discarded thing.

It was *wet* inside, which meant whoever he'd surprised earlier had been heading toward the cabin with water. For what, he could only guess—wash, cook, drink—it wasn't really important. What was important was that this stranger was treating Cade's property as his own.

That wouldn't happen again. Cade didn't need guns to take care of himself, he had two hands and a well-used sense of survival. The squatter had no idea who he was up against.

Although he didn't particularly want to, Cade headed into Eustace, the spot that passed for a town in the middle of nowhere. Before he truly settled in, he wanted to have enough staples to get him by for at least a month. It was early November, but winter was already muscling its way in and he wanted to be prepared to last out the season in his cabin, alone. Since he had to leave behind his well-known horse in Wyoming, along with his sanity, he had picked up a new gelding along the way. As he rode through the woods, he repeated Cade's history to himself. Not that anyone would ask, but he wasn't about to trip over a lie of his own making.

By the time he'd ridden the two hours into town, the sun had warmed up enough that he could no longer see his breath. That would be a rarity within a couple of weeks.

Eustace wasn't much more than a mining town with a dozen wooden buildings, the last stop before travelers tackled the mountains. A saloon, a post office inside the general store, and a few houses were the only buildings in town aside from a lumbermill. From what he'd been told, the mill supplied timber downstate and kept the town going.

The other thing he noticed was the lack of a jail or a sheriff's office. That pleased Cade quite a bit. He didn't need any nosey lawman making his life difficult.

He hoped the store wouldn't overcharge for supplies as many stores that catered to miners often did. Cade didn't want to make a bad impression by arguing. Hell, he didn't want to make *any* impression. The less folks remembered him, the better.

No one greeted him, although there were several folks going about their business in Eustace. Cade dismounted and secured his horse to the hitching post, surprised to find his stomach uneasy.

There was nothing to worry about unless he tripped up on his own tongue. With a deep breath, he stepped up onto the sidewalk and opened the door marked "Eustace Store and Post Office". A tiny bell above the door sounded in the still air. Cade walked in and immediately knew there were two people in the store—one male and one female. Whoever the man was, he stank as if he hadn't seen soap in a year.

She, however, smelled like roses and flour. Cade spotted both of them by the front counter, staring at him. The woman snatched his breath away. Eyes as bright as bluebonnets, wavy brown hair in a braid that lay on her generous breasts, she stood nearly a head taller than the man in front of her. Startled for the first time in a very long time, Cade simply stared until she raised her eyebrows.

"Can I help you, mister?" Her voice was deeper than most women's, smoky and smooth.

"Who is that, Sabrina? Ya think he come to take my mine?"

Cade finally tore his eyes away from the woman and took a look at the man. He had a balding head with greasy curls sticking every which way. The clothes he wore had seen better days, and his hands clutched a tattered knit cap.

"I don't know who it is, Frenchie, but I'm sure he won't be taking your mine." She quirked the corner of her mouth at Cade. "Will you, mister?"

Cade touched the brim of his hat with two fingers in greeting. "Not here to take anything from anybody. Just wanting to buy some supplies."

The woman, Sabrina, patted the man on his shoulder. "See, he's not going to take your mine."

"Hmph, I ain't trusting nobody, nohow. 'Cept you a'course." He smiled at her, showing a smattering of yellowed teeth that would rival any dog's.

As Sabrina smiled back, an arrow of pure lust slammed into Cade's gut. He shook off the feeling with effort. There was no way in hell he could afford to be pining after a woman in town, much less a respectable one. Unless he was paying for it, there'd be no bed play for him no matter how much he was attracted.

"Help yourself to what you need." Sabrina gestured around the store with her arm. "I've got most everything, but I also have the Sears catalog if you've got something special you need."

"Thank you, ma'am." Cade forced himself to walk to the left, out of her line of vision. Jesus H. Christ, he was making a mess of his first day of life.

Focusing on what he needed helped to keep his mind off Sabrina. He gathered some canned goods, coffee, flour and other food items before he went to put everything on the counter. That proved to be his next mistake.

Up close, her rose scent surrounded him, yanked at his dick and nearly knocked him to his knees. It had obviously been too long since he'd been with a woman if he reacted like an idiot to a storekeeper in the middle of nowhere. He didn't need to be involved with a woman, especially one who affected him so strongly and so instantly. Sabrina could make him forget who he was and who he was supposed to be.

She glanced down at the supplies. "Did you need anything else? We've got pots, pans and the like, plus clothing. And"—her gaze roamed over his shoulders—"I think I have a few things in stock that'd fit you."

When her blue gaze collided with his, a beat of pure energy shot between them. He knew she felt it too when her eyes widened. It was the strangest thing he'd ever felt, and it scared the hell out of him.

"No, nothing else." He had to get out of there right fast.

"You need some trousers," a voice piped up from beside him.

Cade had almost forgotten the stinky little man. "What's that?"

Frenchie pointed at Cade's legs. "Your trousers is too short. That ain't gonna do you no good when the snow hits."

Cade could've smacked himself for not even thinking of making sure his pants were the right size. When he accepted them from his friend Brett, he hadn't checked the length. He and Brett were about the same height, but apparently Cade's legs were longer. Ignoring the observant fool, Cade gestured to the food.

"How much do I owe you, ma'am?"

"Two dollars and forty-two cents. I've got some extra sacks from Frenchie's apples. Do you need one?"

She was smart too, dammit. She'd added up the cost

of the goods in her head.

"That'd be fine. Thank you." Cade forced himself to count out the money from his pocket and ignore the living, breathing distraction in front of him. When he was in better control of his emotions, he'd come back and buy pants that actually fit.

"Are you new in town?" Sabrina finished putting everything in the potato sack. He hoped like hell it didn't smell like Frenchie—could be why she was giving them away.

"Yeah, I bought Harmon's place. Name's Cade Brody."

"I wondered if someone would buy Old Louie's place. Pleased to meet you, Mr. Brody. I'm Sabrina Edmonds. My sister and I run the store." She held out her hand and Cade had no choice but to shake it. It was firm, soft, yet had the marks of a woman who worked for a living. It fit perfectly in his palm, and he pulled his hand away as quickly as he could. "If any mail comes in for you, I'll keep it until you get into town."

"Don't expect to get any mail." He looked in her eyes, willing her to let him be.

After a pregnant pause, she smiled again. "Well, then, we're usually here and we live upstairs so if you knock on the door loud enough, we'll hear you."

Cade had to almost kick himself to stop imagining where she slept, which apparently lay just above them. Sabrina was dangerous to his sanity, and he'd do best to keep his distance from her. With a nod to both of them, Cade got out of there like someone was chasing him, his body still thrumming from touching her hand.

Dammit.

Sabrina stared after the stranger, a low arousal pleasantly buzzing through her. She'd seen him when he rode into town, and the man definitely knew how to sit on a horse. The clothes he wore weren't the right size and he looked downright uncomfortable in them. If she had to hazard a guess, he was hiding from something or somebody.

Cade Brody was a handsome man with wavy black hair, and those dark eyes could keep her dreams full for weeks. She didn't normally react so swiftly to a man, but she had this time. He obviously didn't want to answer any questions about himself or his life so she hadn't pushed. However, the feel of his hand lingered on hers like a ghost touch.

"Where'd he come from?" Frenchie scowled at the closed door.

"I don't know. He's just a new neighbor. Be nice," she scolded. "Don't be driving folks away from my store or I'll lose so much business I'll have to close up."

The panic on Frenchie's face almost made her laugh. She'd only meant to tease him, not send him into apoplexy.

"I'll be good, I swear, Sabrina."

"I know you will. Now get on with you over to the bathhouse. You promised me you'd go when you were in town." Sabrina seemed to be the only one who could convince the old miner he needed soap at least a few times a year.

"Okay." Frenchie looked like a reluctant child rather than a sixty-year-old man. "But I ain't gonna like it."

"I already knew that." Sabrina laughed as he dragged his feet leaving the store.

"Who was that?" Ellen appeared in the doorway to the stairs, hovering in the shadows as usual.

"Frenchie." Sabrina shook her head. "Hopefully some lye soap will do some good."

"No, not him. The other man." Ellen watched the comings and goings of the store from a second-story window. After being scarred five years earlier, she spent her time hiding from anyone who might look at her. She had taken care of their invalid mother until she'd passed away the previous year. No matter what Sabrina tried, Ellen adamantly refused to come out of hiding.

"His name is Cade Brody, says he bought Harmon's place." His name even tasted intriguing.

"He's dangerous and dark." Ellen cradled her stomach. "I don't like him."

Sabrina frowned. "You could tell that from behind a window one story up? Ellen, if you're not willing to actually talk to people, don't judge them."

"I'm not judging him. It's just a...feeling I had. I don't think he can be trusted." Ellen sounded hurt.

"I'm sorry, El, I didn't mean to snap." She walked over and gave her younger sister a quick hug, the petite blonde's head barely brushing Sabrina's chin. "I don't know if Mr. Brody can be trusted either, but I doubt he'll be in town very often. I think he's here to hide, from what I don't know."

Ellen touched Sabrina's cheek with her hand. "Be careful, Brina."

Sabrina shook off her sister's concern. They survived their father's death, their mother's sickness, more shysters than they could count, and the groping hands of thousands of miners and lumberjacks, not to mention betrayal and murder as well. One dark-eyed man wasn't going to pose much of a threat.

Cade stared at the Eustace saloon, aptly named Last Gate. He clenched his horse's reins in his fist, the bite of the leather keeping him cognizant of his surroundings. The thirst roared like a monster within him, pulsing a beat in tune with his heart.

Thump, thump, thump.

Deep inside, he knew that one drink would push him back into the blackness he'd fought against for so long. A blackness that had nearly destroyed him. He licked his lips, almost tasting the amber liquid. As he turned away from the saloon, a sound burst from his throat, a cry of desperation or a howl of hunger, he wasn't sure which.

It took every inch of restraint to not turn back to the saloon.

"It's not that bad, *amigo*."

Cade turned and again reached for the gun that didn't

sit at his hip anymore. *Son of a bitch.* A dark-haired man stood before him, hands raised in surrender, but his gaze flickered to Cade's hand as it grasped air. Surely of Mexican descent, the stranger was at least ten years younger than Cade, and sported an amused grin.

After taking a deep breath, he slid his iron self-control into place. He didn't like the fact the stranger had seen him at a low point, when his control had almost shattered. After straightening his hat, he finally met the stranger's gaze.

"You startled me." The words were forced out through his teeth. Cade realized the man could be a threat if he wanted since he was big enough, but he had no weapon and didn't do anything other than smile.

"I can see that." The man held out his hand. "Antonio Rodriguez. I own the Last Gate."

Cade shook hands with the man, feeling hard-won calluses and a firm grip. "Cade Brody, new town idiot."

Antonio laughed. "You were looking at the saloon like it was gonna bite you."

"Nah, just keeping the demons away." Cade let out a shaky breath. The trip to Eustace was turning out to be mistake after mistake.

"Suit yourself." Antonio gestured to the building behind him. "I've got some coffee on and at this time of day, there's nobody else inside."

Cade knew he shouldn't, really shouldn't, but he also knew the rest of the day held nothing but work at the new cabin. A good cup of coffee would be a welcome change from his own brew that resembled sludge.

"Sounds good." Before he could change his mind, Cade stepped toward the saloon and secured his horse to the hitching post.

Antonio walked inside, leaving Cade alone. The hum of the saws in the mill, a horse's whinny and his own heartbeat were the only sounds around him. He licked his lips again and swallowed. Time to test his limits and perhaps make a new acquaintance in town.

The inside of the saloon was nothing unusual. Tables, chairs, a pinewood bar with some rickety stools in front of it. The floor was littered with peanut shells but at least his boots didn't stick. Although Antonio was nowhere to be seen, the atmosphere wasn't threatening and it didn't smell like stale whiskey.

Cade always trusted his first judgment. Last Gate was a safe place, even though it held the one thing that could easily send Cade back into a black pit. Antonio came back carrying two tin cups and a coffeepot with a towel. He poured the steaming brew and set the pot on the towel. Cade took a sip of the black liquid, and his entire body sighed. He hadn't had good coffee like that in months, not since he left Wyoming.

"Good coffee." He almost burned his mouth on the next gulp.

"Thanks. I had to learn how to make it when the only woman that worked here refused to do it anymore." Antonio laughed. "*Mi madre* can be tough."

Cade looked around and noted the polished wood, the

neat bottles behind the bar and the clean glasses. There was definitely a female here. If it was Antonio's mother, then she was a very particular woman. Antonio didn't strike Cade as a man under his mother's thumb, but it was possible.

"We came from Mexico when I was ten. Mamá and I worked here for twelve years until the owner died. He had always loved her so he left the saloon to her." Antonio shrugged. "Now I run it for her and offer strangers hot coffee."

It surprised Cade that Antonio didn't ask any questions about him. Smart man.

"Appears you're doing a good job at it." Cade let the hot coffee warm him, calm him as he sat in companionable silence with Antonio.

"Thanks, *amigo*. I've got some cornbread in the back too. Interested?"

Cade's stomach growled. "I'd pay for good cornbread."

"Good. If I don't charge you, Mamá won't be happy." Antonio disappeared in the back again, leaving Cade alone.

As he glanced around, Cade realized he finally felt comfortable in his surroundings, at least for two minutes. It was a two hour ride back to the cabin, and he needed to be on the way within the next hour, but for now, he wanted to drink coffee and eat cornbread. He pulled four bits from his pocket and put it on the bar.

Relaxing at the saloon with Antonio was a pleasant way to spend an hour. By the time Cade left the Last

Gate, he decided that while Antonio might not be a friend, he was a good contact in Eustace. Cade would do well to remember that.

His last stop in town was the lumbermill. He wanted to build a corral for his horse instead of housing him in the lean-to. The thing had seen at least two or three decades and it leaned more than it should. He'd had plenty of practice mending fences in Wyoming and could swing a hammer with confidence.

Or at least enough to put in some nails and make a corral his horse would be secure in. Cade didn't have many skills that most men had, but he could call himself a cowboy. Perhaps one day he might even get a few cattle on his property.

"Like hell." Cade laughed at his own joke, earning a suspicious glance from the two men loading lumber into a wagon.

"Afternoon, gentlemen." He dismounted and secured his horse, very aware of the stares around him. Previously, people wouldn't have stared at him, but since he'd shed his guns, he was just a tall skinny man with a bad attitude.

He'd never amounted to much more than that anyway.

"Can I help ya?"

Cade turned to find a red-haired man in a flannel shirt and denims standing in front of the mill. The expression on the stranger's face was as bland as oatmeal.

"I need to buy some lumber for a corral, about twenty feet square." Cade had an idea of what it should look like but to be safe, he ordered a bit more than he needed. He was bound to make a few mistakes, although he'd cut out his own tongue before admitting that to anyone.

The redheaded man glanced at the horse and raised a brow. "You got a wagon?"

"No, but I can rent one, I think. There a livery in town?" Cade hadn't considered how to get the wood back to the ranch. Stupid, stupid, stupid. Made him look like the village idiot again.

"Nope, there ain't. Where you live?"

"Livingston Valley." Cade still felt odd saying he had a place to call home, much less one with such a fancy name.

"For an extra five dollars, we can deliver the lumber out there for ya." With a throat clearing to rival any sailor, the redhead spat a nice wad of snot on the cold, dark dirt between them.

Five dollars was goddamn robbery. Cade forced a small smile while he swallowed the urge to show the fool exactly who he was fucking with. "That'd work just fine."

After stepping inside to finalize the order, Cade left the lumbermill with all his good feelings about Eustace gone. Antonio had been a welcome surprise, the rest of town hadn't been.

Except Sabrina of course. She hadn't been a surprise, more like a dangerous distraction he'd do best to avoid.

Chapter Two

Cade headed back to the cabin with his supplies strapped to the horse in sacks. The warmth of the day and a full belly improved his disposition, after he'd forced himself to forget the fool at the lumbermill. His gaze scanned the trail around him as he rode along, never once relaxing his guard. He didn't know the New Mexico territory very well and didn't trust even a flea on a dog's ass.

By the time he reached home, the midday heat had started to wane. The sun was setting, and the evening bite of cold began to nibble at him. Cade ignored the discomfort as he always did. He'd spent too many nights in mud, on rocks or knee-deep in snow.

The closer he got to the cabin, the more the back of his neck itched. Someone was watching him. He cursed the fact that his only weapon was a rifle in its scabbard. If he still had his pistols...but no, he wasn't that person anymore. He was Cade Brody.

By the time his new home was in sight, the itch had turned into an all-out rash.

"Fucking squatter." He finally scratched, only to have

the itch slide down his back too.

The damn thing was, he could not spot whoever was out there. The watcher had to be in the trees to the right, but the man was good, too good. More than likely had been living in the woods for years and knew it like the back of his hand. Nobody else would be so stealthy. Of course, it didn't bode well for Cade's plan to find out whoever the son of a bitch was if he couldn't find him.

He dismounted in front of the cabin, deliberately taking his time unloading the horse, letting his unwanted visitor see how many supplies he'd purchased. Cade was there for good, not just for a week. When the new lumber got delivered next week, he'd have enough to build the corral and hopefully patch up a few holes he'd seen in the walls and floor.

It took Cade ten minutes to see the unwelcome surprise. Lying in front of the fireplace was a rabbit, gutted and ready to be cooked, laid out like a Christmas feast. He spun around, expecting to see the last two seconds of his life with a gun pointed at him, but there was nothing there. He closed the door and approached the offering. A careful scrutiny of the carcass and fireplace revealed no trap. Cade snorted at the empty room around him.

"Think I'm going to believe we're friends now? I don't fucking think so. Must take me for a fool."

He picked up the carcass by its foot and carried it outside. As he walked toward the trees, he shouted to the leaves above.

"I ain't eating nothing you leave behind, squatter. Probably put some poison on it so I'll keel over and leave the nice, warm cabin for you." He threw the rabbit to the foot of the tallest pine. "Eat it yourself."

Expecting an attack, his muscles tensed like iron as he made his way back to the cabin. In another lifetime, he never would have turned his back on an enemy, ever. However, now that he'd been reborn, he found himself doing things, stupid things, like showing his vulnerable, unarmed back to a stranger.

He shook with the urge to tear the trees apart leaf by leaf until he found the bastard. Cade needed to fight, to feel some pain to feel alive. He swallowed the dryness in his mouth as need almost overwhelmed him. God, in a second he'd be running back to the spot he'd buried the damn guns just to feel the cold metal on his skin.

What the hell was wrong with him? Why couldn't he be normal enough to exist each day without death around him?

He'd had a brief taste of what actual life was while he'd lived in Cheshire, Wyoming. It had scared the hell out of him.

Morning brought bright sunshine and the reminder that Cade was completely alone, again. Only this time, he'd chosen the place deliberately, somewhere he could live in peace. Or at least try to.

He rose from the floor and scratched at the union suit that covered him. Dang thing felt odd but it had kept him warm the night before. The fire had gone out and there was no more wood inside the house, of course.

"Remember to stock up on the wood each night, fool." He opened the door and was struck by the beauty of the valley as it sparkled in the sunlight, covered with frost. For just a moment, he simply stood and looked his fill. It was a perfect way to start the day.

However, the rabbit bones on his front step were not. Cade was speechless as he stared down at the gnawed remains of the rabbit, more than likely the same one he'd thrown back to the squatter. The man had a set of brass balls leaving this on Cade's step. Did he think somehow he'd be miraculously trusted by showing he'd eaten the damn rabbit?

Cade kicked the bones aside with one bare foot and grimaced as the cold pieces of gristle slid between his toes. The frost he walked through had him forgetting about the nasty rabbit after his feet turned blue. Next time, he'd not only remember the wood, but boots.

Living without creature comforts sucked.

Sabrina dreamed of the stranger. When she opened her eyes in the gray light of dawn, she gasped as the remnants of sleep slipped away. It had been an unusual night fraught with strange images and erotic thoughts. She'd been widowed for more than five years, five long years without a man in her bed. Apparently her body craved what she couldn't have—Cade Brody.

Even now her pussy pulsed with the memory of what the dream-Cade had done to her, with her. Even her nipples were still rock hard beneath her flannel nightdress. Although she'd probably be late and hear about it all day from Ellen, Sabrina couldn't stop her hand from sliding beneath the cotton to the hungry flesh that needed a release.

The other hand crept to her aching nipples, tweaking and pinching in rhythm with the pleasure she gave herself in the moist folds between her legs. She spread them wider, giving access to her fingers to slide in and out. She closed her eyes and imagined it wasn't her hand pressing against her and into her.

It was him.

A dark man with the darkest eyes who seemed to see beyond her storekeeper's façade to the woman who lurked beneath. His lips were full and even, framing a shining set of teeth that could nibble on her even as his hands pleasured her below.

"*Yessss.*"

Tingles raced up and down her skin as her hands moved faster, pleasure ricocheting through her. She forgot about getting up and making breakfast, or opening the store. Everything slipped from her mind except for the need sinking its claws into her skin. Cade should be here in her bed with his long-fingered hands and lean hips, plunging into her even as she thrust up to meet him.

Her orgasm started at her center and radiated out

through her body as she bucked beneath the covers. Sabrina bit her lip to keep the cry of bliss from escaping into the cold, empty room. This moment was hers and hers alone.

As the pulses faded, she opened her eyes again and saw a widow's room. A small photograph from her wedding day mocked her from its position on the dresser. Eric had been a good man, a solid, steady man who wanted nothing more than to be a good husband. Too bad death had other ideas for him, losing his life at the tender age of twenty-one.

Sabrina sighed. Real life didn't include fantasies about the newest resident in the area, even if he inspired hot, melting dreams.

Ellen entered the room without knocking, thankfully after the self-pleasuring had concluded. "Sabrina, why are you still in bed? I heard a customer rattling the door already."

"It's cold out there." Sabrina forced a smile to her lips. "I was hoping you'd already have the coffee on."

"Please, Brina, you know I don't work in the store while it's open." Ellen glanced out the window. "It's past dawn already."

With that, her sister left the room, and Sabrina bit her tongue. She tried to be patient, but sometimes, like that morning, it was exceptionally hard. Every single day of their lives for the last five years, Sabrina had opened the store. Ellen hid upstairs working on the books and rarely entered the store when it was open. For once, she'd appreciate Ellen opening the store and giving Sabrina time to wake up before she had to be a shopkeeper.

Some days, she wanted to shake her younger sister, then kick her into the bright light of the main street of Eustace. Of course, Sabrina would never be that cruel. Although life had not turned out rosy for Ellen, she'd chosen to be a hermit who watched the world through glass.

Her morning pleasure forgotten, Sabrina climbed out of bed with a frown and a humph at the cold floor that assaulted her feet. No matter what she wanted to be doing, it was time to start the day in earnest.

A few hours later, Sabrina's mood had not improved much. Two miners had refused to pay their bills, half the eggs were broken by a clumsy fool, and someone stole a tin of her best pipe tobacco. Her patience had worn thin, and the last thing she needed was Ellen complaining about the cost of supplies from Santa Fe.

"I swear, the only thing worse than a thief is a thief who claims he's only doing business." Ellen frowned at the invoices in her hands. "It's legal thievery, that's what it is."

The bell over the door tinkled, and Ellen disappeared in a flash behind the curtain. Sabrina muttered, "Thank God," hoping her next customer wouldn't make her bad day even worse.

It was Cade.

A whoosh of pure arousal slammed into her, turning her knees to jelly, setting her heart to racing like a horse.

Holy Mary, she hadn't expected that or him. After all, they'd barely spoken two dozen words to each other. And yet she'd had the most erotic dream of her life about him, and the same day, there he was, in the flesh.

Oh, what flesh it was. Sabrina couldn't stop herself from drinking in every inch of the man, from his ill-fitting brown pants to his lean hips and wide chest. He was a fine specimen of a man. Very, very fine.

"Good morning, Mr. Brody." Curses, her voice sounded high and breathy. "I didn't expect to see you so soon."

"I didn't expect to be back in Eustace so soon. I, uh, need a pair of boots, good boots that'll hold up against snow and the like." He glanced down at the worn shoes with the big heel at the back. They looked like they belonged on a city street rather than a rough town. "These ain't fit for a mountain winter."

His long legs drew her gaze as did what lay between them. Before she embarrassed herself, Sabrina headed over to the shoes, hoping like hell they had a pair in his size. After a moment or two of fumbling like a blushing schoolgirl, she found several pairs of sturdy boots that might fit his large feet.

He'd come up close behind her, nearly blocking the light from the window. His presence filled the air around them, taking the breath right out of her. She looked into his dark eyes and saw more than she expected, ancient pain and a loneliness so deep it appeared bottomless.

Cade Brody certainly wasn't a simple miner or

mountain man. If she had to hazard a guess, he was a man who'd made some bad choices in his life that were currently riding his back. Sabrina blinked and forgot she was holding boots or even why she'd walked over to that side of the store.

They gazed into each other's souls for a timeless moment, sharing themselves. For her, it was a relief for someone to see everything she hid. Most days she simply accepted that no one would ever want to know what lurked beneath the efficient shopkeeper. Today she opened herself up and allowed a perfect stranger to see her unhappiness, her discontent, her yearning.

The air between them crackled as the moment stretched on, threatening to snap. He reached up, fingers inches away from her skin. Sabrina leaned toward him, knowing how his hand would feel before flesh touched flesh.

"Sabrina?" Ellen's voice startled her so badly, she dropped the boots.

All three pair fell towards Cade's feet. Sabrina had counted herself as well versed in human behavior, especially being around so many people, but Mr. Brody surprised the heck out of her when he caught the boots. No, not caught, he *snatched* them out of the air so fast she barely saw him move until the shoes were clutched in his hands.

She stared at him in astonishment, gazing from his face to the boots. "Sweet heavens, I've never seen the like." Her father's brogue popped out of her mouth before she thought about it.

Cade looked almost as shocked as she felt. He set the boots down on the table beside them and stepped away from her. Ellen came around the corner and stopped short when she caught sight of him.

Sabrina frowned at her. "Ellen, this is Mr. Brody. Mr. Brody, this is my sister, Ellen."

"Sister? Ah, yes I remember you mentioning her." He cocked his head in Ellen's direction as if he were studying her. She squirmed in place, sliding backwards even as Sabrina shook her head no. "It's a pleasure to meet you, Miss Edmonds."

"O'Neill." Ellen surprised Sabrina by speaking. "It's Miss O'Neill."

Cade's head whipped back and he stared hard at Sabrina. "And your name is Edmonds?"

He was asking her if she was married without actually forming the question. She ought to make him feel guilty or at least tell him it wasn't his business, however two minutes ago she'd been about to kiss him. Sabrina was nothing if not honest with herself and that was the truth.

"Yes, Mrs. Edmonds." She swallowed the memory of Eric that threatened to make her day dark again. "My husband died five years ago."

Sabrina had no idea if it was relief on Cade's face or annoyance that he didn't know she was a widow.

"My condolences."

"Thank you." Clearing her throat, Sabrina looked at

Ellen. "Did you need me for something?"

"Oh, I almost forgot. Mr. Oleson delivered the load from Phoenix." Ellen kept her face averted from Cade. Sabrina wished she could convince her sister that a scar on her face didn't matter a whit to anyone but herself. "We can close the store and inventory it as soon as you're done with Mr. Brody." With a quick nod, she disappeared back behind the curtain.

"Your sister doesn't favor you." Cade stared after Ellen.

Sabrina expected the familiar observation. "Yes, I've realized that," she said dryly. "My father was a tall Irishman while my mother was small and blonde like Ellen."

Cade's gaze swung to hers. "Your father was blessed."

She didn't know how to respond to his obscure comment. Was he saying she was beautiful or that her mother was her father's blessing? Sabrina wanted to ask but didn't because he started examining the boots, breaking the awkward moment in two.

"You probably want to get some trousers too." She put the table between them, able to take a deep breath for the first time since he walked in the store. As she examined the neatly stacked clothing in front of her, she heard him pull off his odd shoes and slip on the boots. He repeated it several times while she tried her damnedest to focus on picking trousers for him.

Cade was slender with long legs, obviously too long for the trousers he was wearing. After a few minutes of mad scrambling, she found one black pair and one dark blue pair. When she held them up for him to see, he'd picked the boots that fit and was simply staring at her.

"You're nervous." Cade sounded surprised.

Nothing like being blunt but Sabrina could be blunt too. "You're overwhelming."

He smiled, flashing white teeth that hit her like a blow to the stomach. The man was handsome, but smiling, he was blindingly beautiful.

"I guess we're at odds then, aren't we?" He pointed at the trousers. "I'll take those and the boots."

Sabrina felt off-kilter by Cade, and it annoyed her. She didn't like being out of control for any reason, and his presence alone, not to mention his off-color comments, made that control slip.

"Fine. Let me tally these up so you can be on your way."

Cade nodded and meandered toward the meager supply of books she had. Antonio bought them almost as soon as they came in, as did Melissa Fuller, the daughter of Sam the lumbermill owner. The only ones left were on horse husbandry, a seed catalog and a book of poems by Shakespeare. Even Melissa didn't want them. Sabrina remembered a miner ordering the book for his pregnant wife, but she died before the book came in.

Perhaps it was cursed. Interestingly enough, Cade picked up the book of poems and started reading.

Damn the man, he seemed to be deliberately annoying her now. She slammed the trousers on the counter and wrapped them in brown paper so fast, she gave herself three paper cuts. Cursing under her breath, she wrapped the twine with a snap. When she looked up, he had his nose buried in the book and wasn't even paying attention to her snit.

Sabrina needed to forget about him, so she did what she did best, focused on being a shopkeeper. She added up his purchases, a nice bit of money to add to the till.

"That'll be six dollars and seventy-five cents, Mr. Brody."

Silence met her request. When she glanced up, he read on, oblivious to her and everything around him.

"Should I add in the book too?"

Cade glanced up, a guarded expression on his face. "The book?" He looked down as if the book had suddenly appeared in his hands. "It's better than talking to the trees I guess. Sure, I'll take the book too."

"Tell you what, that book's been sitting there for two years. Consider it a welcome gift. Just pay me for the boots and trousers." Sabrina just wanted him out of there, regardless of how attracted she was to him. Cade seemed to sense it because he paid her quickly and took his package.

"Much obliged, Mrs. Edmonds."

"Good day, Mr. Brody." Stilted conversation for an awkward moment, but Sabrina couldn't seem to bring herself to do anything else.

With a nod, he finally left the store. She stared at the closed door and wondered what had just happened, then mentally slapped herself for hoping he'd come back soon.

Cade left the general store as if his ass were on fire. It sure as hell felt like the rest of him was. Jesus, Mary and Joseph, what just happened in there? He went from buying boots to almost fucking Sabrina right there on the notions table and then walking out with a book of Shakespeare's poems in his hand.

He shook his head to clear it, but it didn't do any good. The voluptuous shopkeeper had knocked him sideways and he couldn't seem to find his balance.

"Did Mrs. Edmonds convince you to buy that book?"

Cade looked up to see a young girl peering at the book in his hand. She was probably no more than sixteen with frizzy brown hair and dark green eyes. Kind of plain, but her face reflected deep intelligence and sass he recognized well. Reminded him a bit of a certain redhead he knew in Wyoming named Adelaide Malloy.

"No, I wanted the book. She didn't convince me of anything." Except how long it had been since he'd bedded a woman.

"You read Shakespeare then?" The girl sauntered toward him, hands clasped behind her back. She wore a conservative dark blue dress, much too staid for a young girl so obviously full of life. He smiled when he saw she sported mud on her fancy boots all the way up to her ankles.

"When I've a mind to." He tucked the book into his saddlebags along with the paper-wrapped trousers, another unplanned purchase.

"I prefer his plays to his poetry, there's a lot more sex in them."

Cade choked on his own spit as she walked past him toward the store. "You've got quite a mouth on you, girl."

"You have no idea, mister." For a moment, she looked much older than she was. Cade had a feeling this little spitfire gave her parents more than they bargained for.

"You'd best be careful who you throw those words at. Some fella who ain't as nice as me is gonna take that the wrong way." Cade knew the type of man of whom he spoke. He'd run into too many of them growing up with his pack of mothers.

The girl waved her hand in dismissal. "Oh, I don't think I have anything to worry about. My daddy owns Eustace and there's no one in town who'd dare harm a hair on my head."

Cade laughed without humor. "I wasn't talking about somebody you knew. I mean, you don't know me, do you?" When he stepped toward her, a flash of real fear zipped through her eyes, then it was gone.

"You read poetry. I'm not particularly afraid of men who read poetry no matter how mean or frightening they look." She stuck her freckled nose in the air. "You're just trying to scare me."

He didn't know whether to be amused or annoyed at the little female. It wasn't his business if she went around sassing every man alive. She was her father's problem, not his.

"Be on your way, little girl. I don't have time to jaw with you anymore." Cade turned his back and started tying his useless boots to the saddle. Never thought slipping on his ass in the mud that morning would've brought him back to Eustace and confounded by one female.

And annoyed by a smaller one.

"Where are you going?"

"Home." He pulled the rope tight then put his foot in the stirrup to mount up.

"You can't leave yet. I don't even know your name." The little booger grabbed hold of the horse's reins and hung on like a green-eyed cocklebur.

"You haven't used your manners either. Most folks are polite enough to introduce themselves before they start asking a million questions." Cade frowned at her, willing the girl to find someone else to bother.

Pink stained her cheeks, but to her credit she didn't lower her gaze. "You're right, of course. I'm Miss Melissa Fuller."

He sighed heavily. "Cade Brody. Now be on your way, Miss Fuller. There must be other people in this town you can annoy."

She grinned and released the reins. "Not at the moment. You are new and therefore interesting."

For some insane reason, he felt the urge to grin back at her. What the hell had Sabrina done to him?

"Well, I've got things to do so I'm leaving." The lame

excuse sounded so stupid, he almost winced when it fell out of his mouth.

She cocked one brown eyebrow. "You've got things to do in your brand-new boots?" Pointing at his old shoes hanging from the saddle, she tsked. "Look at those. What are you, Mr. Brody, a gambler?"

"No, I'm not a gambler, and I'm done playing with you." This time when he threw himself up in the saddle she didn't try to stop him.

"A gunslinger then."

Cade's body tensed as tight as a guitar string, but he kept his face neutral. "I think you've been reading too many books. Good day, Miss Fuller."

She curtseyed. "Pleasure to meet you."

He might have grinned at her precociousness, but the little imp was like a woodpecker. Relentlessly pecking at him until he'd do something stupid like tell her about the dead man he'd buried in the woods.

Chapter Three

"Who's Cade Brody?"

Sabrina looked up from her dinner at Wylie's Restaurant to find Sam Fuller standing over her table, frowning. Ten years her senior, he was a widower who'd done his best to convince Sabrina to marry him. She'd refused so many times, it had almost become a routine for them. For the last two years, each Sunday he arrived with a bouquet of some kind of flowers, chatted with her mother when she was alive, then spent the next hour on the porch with Sabrina. He was handsome, tall with curly brown hair and kind eyes. However, there was absolutely no spark between the two of them. Sabrina couldn't even imagine kissing him much less bedding him.

Even so, he ended Sundays by asking, "Well, you think you and me might get hitched this week?"

Sabrina always turned him down, but considered Sam a friend. He was religiously devoted to his daughter and treated her as if she would remain a little girl forever. Melissa took every opportunity to show her father he was wrong. His view on the world was quite different than Sabrina's in that respect.

"He's nobody."

Oh, now that was a big, fat lie. She hoped her cheeks weren't advertising her disingenuous behavior.

"Well *nobody's* got Melissa chatting like a magpie. I can't seem to shut her up about him. He the type of man who'd take advantage of young girls?" Sam sat down with a thump in the chair across from her, without permission, which told Sabrina he was truly worried.

After setting down her fork, she took a deep breath before answering. "I've had two conversations with him. I'd say in my opinion he is a decent sort of fellow, but a little out of place in the wilds of New Mexico. Didn't even have a good pair of boots or trousers when he arrived."

That brought up images of Mr. Brody's behind, and she bit her tongue to will the image away.

"Where'd he come from?" Sam leaned toward her, seemingly intent on finding out everything he could while Sabrina ate her dinner.

"Do you mind if I finish my meatloaf before the interrogation?" She smiled tightly. "I treat myself once a week to dinner out on Fridays and I don't want to offend you, but it's getting cold." Wylie's always had good eats, and meatloaf was one of her favorites. She and Eric used to have supper together there, and after he was gone, Sabrina continued the tradition, if only to feel as though she had something in her life other than the store.

Sam glanced at her plate and sighed. "I can't believe I just did that. You must think I'm a horse's ass. Please let me pay for your meal."

Sabrina held up her hand. "No, I can't let you do that. You know how folks talk, Sam. There would be tongues wagging all over the county by tomorrow morning that you and I are courting."

A small flash of pain crossed his features. "I'd be right proud if that did happen."

Patience wearing thin, Sabrina took a bite of her dinner and chose not to answer him. She'd turned him down hundreds of times. There was no reason for him to hold out any hope she'd change her mind now.

It was true that many marriages started out with husband and wife barely knowing each other, only to find love along the way. Sabrina wasn't about to take that chance again, once was enough, and her widowhood gave her certain status and privileges unmarried women didn't get.

Sabrina valued her independence and no matter how much she cared for Sam, she wasn't about to give that up to marry a friend.

"I'll leave you to your meal then. Much obliged if you could stop by the mill to talk when you're done, as long as Ellen doesn't need you." He stood and held his hat in his hands, looking as penitent as he could without being on his knees.

She couldn't possibly stay mad at him. "Of course I'll come by. I'll tell you what I know about Mr. Brody."

Sam nodded and left her alone.

Cade.

Her traitorous body remembered the feel of him

standing inches away, the intricate details of his dark eyes, even the spot on his chin he'd missed shaving that morning. If she wasn't careful, Sabrina could become more than attracted to the stranger.

When she snorted at herself, she almost choked on the gravy.

Fifteen minutes later, Sabrina walked over to the mill. The night air was cold enough that she could see her breath. Shivering, she tightened the brightly colored shawl around her shoulders and berated herself for not wearing the beautiful wool coat she'd splurged on last month. If she'd taken the time to walk back to the store instead of directly to the mill, she could have gotten it.

However, she knew if she went back to the store, more than likely she wouldn't have left again to go see Sam. It wasn't as if the lumbermill was a bad place, but it held such dark memories of Ellen's attack and Eric's death, Sabrina avoided the building as much as she could. The hard-packed dirt beneath her shoes grew softer as she approached the front of the mill, the result of inches of packed sawdust.

By the time she reached the door, Sam had already come out to meet her. He looked apologetic in the purple light of dusk.

"I'm sorry, Sabrina, I should have met you at the store. I know you aren't comfortable coming in—"

Sabrina waved her hand. "It's okay. I need to stop being foolish about the mill." It would be hard, but she'd accomplished harder tasks. Confronting ghosts was messy business.

"It's not foolish. You've got reason to steer clear of a place that holds such bad memories." Sam took her elbow in his hand and led her up the steps. "I appreciate you coming by. This afternoon Melissa started writing her name as 'Mrs. Cody' on her slate." He shook his head. "She's suddenly in love with this stranger, and no matter what I say, she just smiles and keeps on."

She'd had no idea Melissa had formed an infatuation for the dark Mr. Brody already. In fact, Sabrina didn't even know the girl had met Cade.

"He came into town just last week. How did she run into Mr. Brody already?" Shivers ran up and down Sabrina's skin as the smell of wood permeated her nose. Her stomach churned as another shadow danced across her mind. Swallowing hard, she walked into Sam's office and felt grateful when he shut the door behind him.

"I thought it was at the store, but perhaps not. You didn't introduce them?" Sam pulled out the chair beside his desk for Sabrina to sit down.

"No, I didn't." Sabrina wondered how Melissa managed to finagle a meeting with the mysterious Cade. "She's a resourceful girl."

Sam sat down heavily in his chair and pinched the bridge of his nose. "You have no idea."

Sabrina held her breath, hoping like hell he wasn't going to tell her that Cade had done something inappropriate with Melissa. She was just a girl and wasn't yet ready to actually be with a man in earnest. Her encounters should be limited to her imagination.

"What happened?"

Sam slammed his fist onto the desk. "Nothing, as far as I know, yet when I caught her writing Mrs. Melissa Brody today, she told me it was just for fun, as if I believe that." He leaned forward and speared Sabrina with a sharp look. "Now tell me what you know about Cade Brody."

He was being more pushy and aggressive than she'd ever seen him. It was very unlike Sam, which told her this was about more than Melissa's obsession with a stranger.

Sabrina covered his hand with hers. "Sam, what's wrong?"

He closed his eyes. "I can't talk to her anymore. She refuses to even say 'Good morning' or 'Hello' to me. Half the time I don't even know where she is. The men in the lumbermill think she's got a secret beau. No one misses an opportunity to tell me I'll be a grandpappy soon."

"I can hardly believe it." Sabrina knew men sometimes joked with each other but this was going too far. "Why would they do that?"

"I don't know, but I feel like things are out of my control. She's almost a woman and I can hardly stand the thought."

Sabrina couldn't help Sam become a better parent since she had no experience herself. However, she felt obligated to listen because he was her friend.

He looked into her eyes with the saddest gaze she'd

ever seen. "The only good thing in my life is you."

The very last thing she wanted was to give Sam false expectations. She'd turned down Sam's marriage proposals more times than she could count. He couldn't possibly expect she'd up and say yes because he was travelling rough road with his daughter. No one wanted to marry out of pity, least of all Sabrina. She'd married Eric out of friendship and a misplaced sense of rightness. She'd never make a mistake like that again.

"You have a lot of blessings, Sam, not the least of which is a successful business and a beautiful daughter." Sabrina wasn't going to allow Sam to wallow in self-pity.

Sam stood and crossed the room to stare out the window. He let out a sigh, fogging the window with his hot breath against the cool glass. "Sometimes I wonder."

Sabrina wanted to slap her forehead in frustration. Sam was turning into a whiny child and she'd had about enough of it for the evening. "I've got to get back to the store, Sam."

As she walked to the door, he grabbed her arm, his fingers biting into her. Sabrina pulled away from him, then rubbed her skin.

"You hurt me."

He threw his hands in the air and stepped back, anger clearly written on his face. "You're leaving."

"I don't know why you asked me here. I've told you what I know about Cade Brody, which isn't much. You're just going to have to talk to your daughter on your own." She yanked open the door and stormed out, annoyed with her friend.

Cade saw the roots on the ground in front of his door and frowned. His mysterious visitor seemed to think he needed help finding food, which was completely ridiculous. He knew exactly how to ride to Eustace for supplies.

As if he would know what to do with roots anyway. Cade couldn't cook worth a shit, beyond eggs, bacon and beans, so most everything he ate came from a can, a restaurant or a frying pan. He secured his horse in the lean-to behind the house, mumbling to himself about his mysterious visitor. When he got back to the house, he kicked the roots aside.

He stepped through the door and a sharp object smacked him in the back. Cade stumbled and his hands grabbed for the doorjamb. He whirled around and reached for the gun that didn't sit at his hip. *Again.* He straightened and looked down to find another one of those damn roots by his feet.

"You little bastard." Cade stalked outside, snarling, his pride wounded and his back smarting.

"Excuse me, mister."

Cade looked up to find a young man driving a wagon. No more than sixteen, the kid had sprouts of whiskers on his chin, or perhaps they were dirt, mousy brown hair and too-big clothes that looked like they'd been owned by a man twice his size.

"What do you want?" Cade snapped.

"Mr. Fuller sent me up here with some lumber you wanted." To his credit, the kid's voice didn't shake, but he swallowed hard enough to make his Adam's apple bob. "You Mr. Brody?"

"Yeah, that's me." Cade finally noticed the lumber in the back of the wagon. He'd been so distracted by the little shit plaguing him, his powers of observation had been seeing red along with the rest of him.

He couldn't wait to get his hands on the fool in the woods. His hands tightened into fists at the thought. Cade was not a man to be played with, but it appeared to be a lesson he needed to teach.

"Mister?"

"Fine. Get the wood unloaded." Cade stared into the trees, willing himself to see something, anything.

Thumps, grunts and loud bangs came from behind him, but Cade ignored the kid. He worked for Fuller, he could unload the wood alone. When he screeched like a little girl, Cade whipped around to find the kid hopping on one foot, a pile of boards scattered on the ground.

"Jesus H. Christ, what the hell did you do?"

"I slipped." The kid's face bloomed red and sweaty.

Cade didn't want to pay attention to the kid, but he did anyway. A year ago, he would have walked away and left him.

He held the kid's elbow to steady him. The young man was skinny, but wiry and strong.

"Is your foot broken?" Cade tried not to sound

annoyed, but he had no desire to take the delivery boy back to Eustace. He wanted to get to looking in the woods again.

"Might be. It hurts like the dickens."

"Shit." Cade sighed and picked the kid up. "You might as well get in the wagon."

After setting the kid down on the wagon seat, Cade grabbed the rest of the wood and threw it in a pile by the door. He'd have to stack it later, not that he was looking forward to it.

"What's your name?" Cade started examining the kid's foot.

"Jeremiah." The kid closed his eyes tightly, looking for all the world like he was going to fall on his face in the dirt.

"Don't go fainting on me like some girl now." He used his softest touch on the rapidly swelling foot.

"You a sawbones or something?" Jeremiah asked through clenched teeth.

Cade snorted. "Not hardly. I learned a bit in the sal— building I grew up in. Seen a lot of, er, wounds in my time, helped out a doctor a time or two." At least he didn't faint at the sight of blood.

"Is it broke?" Jeremiah peered over the top of his knee at the wound.

"Yep, I think so. Dammit." Cade glared at the woods. "I had something, no *someone* to find this afternoon."

"What?" The kid frowned and glanced at the trees.

"Nothing, just thinking out loud." If he was any kind of neighbor, he'd bring the kid back to town to get his foot looked after. Cade could also wrap the kid's foot up and send him back alone.

What if Jeremiah passed out on the way?

"Shut up," Cade growled at the voice in his head. It had started to sound remarkably like his friend, Brett Malloy, the most honest straight-shooter he'd ever met. Dumb son of a bitch needed to stop reminding Cade of what the right thing to do was. It was high time he made that decision for himself.

"Are you talking to me?" Jeremiah inched back on the seat, setting himself up for a passel of splinters.

"No, someone's been squatting in my cabin." Cade took his neckerchief off and wrapped Jeremiah's foot. "It ain't the cleanest thing in the world but it's all I got besides a blanket, and I don't rightly want to tear that up."

"You seen the ghost?" Jeremiah's flushed face had become as white as milk.

Cade stopped dead and stared at the kid. "Ghost?" What the hell was he talking about?

"Oh yeah, the ghost of Livingston Valley. Old Louie used to tell stories about it. Spooked him something awful." Jeremiah shrank back even further onto the hard seat, looking as if the ghost was about to bite him in the ass.

"There's no such thing as ghosts." Cade frowned. "Whatever Louie told you was whiskey talking, nothing more."

"The ghost is real." Jeremiah sounded like a preacher in church giving a passionate sermon. "One night I seen it out back behind the cabin. Louie had some chili for supper and gave me some. I was leaving and"—he swallowed hard—"it floated right at me screeching like an owl. Had soiled drawers that night, I did."

Cade swallowed the laugh that threatened to escape. It was obvious Jeremiah believed what he was saying, however, Cade didn't. He'd seen and done too much in his life to believe in ghosts, except for the ones that resided inside him.

After he finished wrapping the kid's skinny foot, he noted the pale complexion and shaking hands. There was no way Jeremiah was faking the injury, which meant Cade needed to help him get back into town.

"Be right back." Cade took his time saddling his horse, running over and over in his mind why he came up here into the corner of the world to begin again. It appeared the world didn't want him to stay hidden, rather it wanted him to stay in the light. God knows what Sabrina would think to see him in town yet again, considering he said he hadn't planned on coming into town often. This would be the third time in a week.

Jesus Christ and all the heavenly saints.

Why the hell couldn't things go right, for once? With a sour disposition, Cade cinched the saddle tight on the as-yet-unnamed horse and led him back to the wagon. As he tied off the reins to the back of the wagon, the kid watched him with wide eyes, looking like a damn hoot owl.

Cade climbed up on the hard wooden seat. "Move over." He reluctantly picked up the reins then clicked his tongue at the horses. "Lucky for you somebody taught me how to handle one of these things."

"Are you taking me back to town?"

"That'd be why I'm in the wagon, boy." Cade needed to stop thinking about the upcoming visit to Eustace, so he turned his attention back to what Jeremiah had said. "What did you see?"

"You mean with the ghost?" Jeremiah winced as the wagon bounced over the rutted path.

"Well I don't want to know about your shitty pants." Cade sure as hell didn't want to hear any stories, but maybe the kid could give him a clue about his mysterious visitor. At least that would keep his mind off other things.

"It was dressed something dark, with long white hair like a lady." Jeremiah swallowed so hard, Cade heard his throat slide up and down. "It ran past me so fast, I almost didn't see it. The air behind it smelled like pine so I knew it was the ghost that lived in the woods."

Smelled liked pine?

"What do you mean it smelled?" Cade sat up straighter, now completely interested in the story. Ghosts damn sure didn't smell like anything, that is if they even existed, which they didn't.

"It ran past me fast, but I was born in a mountain cabin, mister, I know what pine smells like." Jeremiah nodded, his foot pain apparently forgotten.

"And you said it had long white hair?"

"Just like an angel." The boy appeared to be half afraid, half in love with the mysterious "ghost".

Cade wondered if the boy was touched in the head. "More like some little shit who thinks it's funny to pester me and scare foolish boys."

"Oh no, sir, it ain't nothing like that. Old Louie said the ghost helped him out once or twice toward the end 'afore he died, like when he couldn't get meat, there'd be a rabbit on the step for him." Jeremiah believed every word he said judging by the earnest expression on his face.

Cade didn't find anything unusual about it. "Sounds like a neighbor helping out."

"You think what you like." Jeremiah stuck his chin out. "I know what I seen."

It's possible that whoever had been helping the old man was the same person harassing Cade now. What would be the purpose though? It wasn't as if Cade was a decrepit old man who shit in his drawers and drooled. He could take care of himself. Living with Brett Malloy for four months had taught him a lot about that very thing.

No self-righteous fool could change that.

"All right, let's say there is a ghost. Why the hell would it throw a turnip at me?" His damn back still smarted from the flying root.

Jeremiah's brows rose so far into the dirt on his forehead, Cade couldn't see them. "It threw a turnip at you? What did you do, mister, call it a devil instead of an angel?"

Cade had a fleeting thought that perhaps the angel knew a devil when he saw one.

By the time they got close to town, Jeremiah had grown even paler and was sweating buckets.

"You okay, boy?" Cade didn't need the boy dying on him after delivering wood for a corral. Jesus, the whole town would likely lynch him.

"Just feel a bit sick to—" With that, Jeremiah leaned over the side of the wagon and tossed up what was left of his last meal.

Cade wrinkled his nose at the smell and his own stomach heaved. Too many memories slammed into him at once, the purple room, the gaudy curtains, a woman cupping his face and telling him it would be all right, then the flash of other faces, smells and times. A bit of gorge crept up his throat and with monumental effort, he swallowed it back and tried to shake off the dark magic on his back. It had been so many years since he'd thought of that place and now it appeared the past was swinging around full circle to his present.

He pinched his fingers in the traces to bring back his self-control.

"I need to drop you off. Where the hell is the doc's place?"

"Ain't no doc." Jeremiah wiped his mouth on his sleeve, the spittle leaving a shine on the rough fabric.

"No doc? Then what do the folks in Eustace do when they're sick?" The image of Alexandra Malloy popped into Cade's head. The beautiful blonde doctor had spoiled all future experiences with any physicians he might meet. However, he was supposed to stop thinking about the past. He couldn't ever go back to see the Malloys because dead men don't visit the living.

"Clara Weathers is the closest thing we got. She delivers all the young'uns and has a good hand at doctoring." Jeremiah pointed with a shaking hand. "Yellow house next to the store."

Of course it was next to the store. Why wouldn't it be? After all, Sabrina must think Cade was a nuisance already, why not make it worse?

With a fierce scowl, Cade stopped the wagon in front of the small house then set the brake. He glanced at the boy and noticed his eyes were starting to roll back in his head.

"Dammit." Cade jumped down and caught Jeremiah in his arms. The kid barely weighed as much as a saddle—Sam Fuller must not pay very much. As Cade walked up to the front door, he wondered if Sabrina was watching, then wanted to kick his own ass for even thinking about her.

"He's a devil, bringing blackness into Eustace."

Sabrina controlled the urge to roll her eyes. "Who's a

devil?" She continued dusting the cans of peaches while she waited for Ellen to continue.

"That stranger. He wears a dark cloak around him as if it's part of his skin. You'd best be careful." Ellen looked away from the window with a frightened gaze.

Sabrina stopped and walked over to where her sister stood. "What are you talking about?" She looked out the window and saw Cade carrying Jeremiah into Clara's house. The boy's foot was wrapped and he was as floppy as a rag doll. Something must've happened to him and Cade had brought the boy into town for help. It confirmed her instincts about him—he was a good man. "Looks to me like he's being a good neighbor and helping Jeremiah. Lord knows not many people do."

Jeremiah was the bastard child of one of the men who worked at the mill. His *mamá* up and died when he was four, leaving a small frightened child behind. Hiram, the father, tried his best, but the man was just not cut out to be a parent. Sam had hired Jeremiah to do odd jobs around the mill and when he got big enough, to deliver lumber. He was still small, but he had the heart of a giant.

"Don't be fooled. That man is darkness come to life." Ellen looked truly afraid as she backed away from the window. "You become someone else when you're near him."

"What does that mean?" Sabrina fidgeted with the rag in her hand, certain she knew exactly what Ellen meant. Mr. Brody seemed to have some kind of magic about him that turned a boring storekeeper into a shameless hussy. Although married women occasionally stepped out with men after they became widowed, it wasn't normal to feel such powerful urges for a man. It couldn't be normal. Even now, when she couldn't see him anymore, Sabrina felt a pulsing heat deep within her at just the thought of him.

She didn't dare mention the dreams to anyone. Each night he came to her, leaving her gasping for release when she woke in sweat-soaked sheets. Sabrina now even slept naked, which seemed to heighten the pleasure with her nocturnal lover. A heat crept across her cheeks at the memory of just how much she looked forward to closing her eyes at night.

Ellen cocked her head. "You carry a warm pink glow around you most times. You're kind and considerate, a good person. Then when I saw you with that man, your glow turned deep purple, almost red, and it scared me."

Sabrina couldn't deny Ellen's assessment, even if it was a bit odd. Mr. Brody did make her feel not normal and if her glow was purple, then so be it. It wasn't as if Sabrina had asked anything to happen between her and Cade, it just did. Something about him called to the woman deep inside her, the wanton who dared to show her face only when no one else could see what she was thinking and doing.

"It's okay, Ellen." Sabrina enfolded her petite sister in a hug. "Mr. Brody is just a customer. He's made it clear he doesn't want to be in Eustace very much. I'm sure only the direst of circumstances brought him back so soon."

Ellen trembled in her arms. "Death follows him like a shadow. Please, Sabrina, you mustn't be near him anymore."

What could she say? Sabrina wasn't near him very much, only in her imaginings. She didn't want to lie to Ellen, but she could not control where her dreams took her. Ever since Ellen had nearly died, and Sabrina's husband had, Ellen had become more than a recluse. The fact was, she almost bled to death and claimed to have seen their father while she was unconscious in Clara's care. After she recovered, Ellen started seeing halos around people that she researched in a book and discovered they were called auras. To her, they were an indicator of a person's inside, good or evil.

"I don't plan on being near him. He's not likely to chase after an old widow like me anyway." Sabrina forced a chuckle then released her sister from her embrace and looked into her wide blue eyes. "Cade Brody is no threat to me or you, I promise."

Ellen nodded, but her eyes revealed her lie. She didn't believe a word Sabrina said.

Chapter Four

"Hello? Who's out there?" a woman called from behind the door.

Cade shifted the dead weight in his arms, sure the boy had doubled his size in the last ten feet to the house. "My name is Cade Brody, ma'am. I've got Jeremiah out here with a broken foot."

The door cracked open a few inches. "Jeremiah Carlton?"

"I guess so. He's a boy around sixteen years old or so." Cade felt a twinge of embarrassment that he knew nothing about the boy in his arms other than his name and that he had an overactive imagination.

"Yep, that'd be Jeremiah Carlton." The door swung wide, and Cade blinked at the woman in front of him.

Growing up in the type of house he did, Cade had seen so many different kinds of women, he'd lost track. Unlike some men, like Brett's brother Trevor, Cade hadn't sampled many of them. The darkness of his childhood made him keep his distance from women until his need overtook his brain. Fortunately or not, his base needs hadn't taken over too often, but when they did, Cade gave the woman twice her rate and gentleness he was sure she'd never received from a customer.

However, his experiences with the female sex didn't help him as he saw Clara Weathers for the first time. She stood no taller than his elbow, a perfectly formed little person from her brown bun of hair to her tiny little hands. He'd heard of small people in circuses, but had never seen one with his own eyes, much less what he thought was a full-grown one.

"Stop gaping, you fool, and bring the boy in. Did he faint?" She waved him in and slammed the door behind them. "This way."

Cade followed like an idiot, sure the expression on his face was one of dumbness with no bounds.

"Well, did he faint?" she demanded as she opened the door to a small room containing a narrow bed covered in white sheets.

"I, uh, yeah, he fainted just as we got here." Cade continued his streak of stupidity by staring at Clara more.

"Would you lay him down on the bed so I can take a look at him, please?" She scowled as Cade put the boy on the bed. "What's the matter, you never see a woman before?"

"Yes, ma'am, I've seen more than my fair share of them since I grew up in a New Orleans bordello." Well, where the hell had that come from? Jesus please us, was he losing his mind? Why would he have told her that?

"Then you've seen plenty. Stop staring and help me get his trousers off so I can get a good look at his foot and leg."

Without a smidge of hesitation, Clara unbuttoned the boy's shirt and took it off, quickly checking him for injuries. Cade lifted Jeremiah so she could slide the trousers off more gently than a butterfly's wing.

"What happened to him?" She untied the bandage and unwound it while she fired questions at Cade. "Were you there? Did you wrap his foot?"

"He dropped some lumber on his foot. Yes, I was there and I wrapped his foot with a neckerchief." Cade took the dirty bandage when she handed it to him.

"You did a good job." The boy's foot had swollen to twice its size, looking like a grotesque parody of a human appendage. "Go out to the well and get me a bucket of the coldest water you can bring up. If there's any icicles on the edge, put those in the water too."

Cade had promised himself never to take orders again from a woman. Since he'd left New Orleans, most of them treated him like a threat, and therefore with detached fear. Clara didn't appear to be afraid of him at all, which was very odd especially considering how tiny she was.

"Go!" Clara shooed him out of the room. "We need to get the swelling down and standing around like an idiot isn't helping."

He blinked and left the room, then found himself standing at the well lowering the bucket before he even knew what he was doing. Some small bits of ice clung to the underside of the stones around the well. After hauling a bucket from the bottom, he broke the ice off and threw it in the already-frigid water.

As he walked back to the house, he couldn't stop himself from glancing at the back of the store. The white lace curtains in the window fluttered as if someone had been looking at him. A thump rolled through him and landed somewhere near his stomach. Was Sabrina or her odd sister watching him? He tried to hide his reaction, but damned if a shiver didn't crawl up his spine. Cade lived in the shadows for a reason, he didn't like to be watched or noticed.

He carried the water to the house too fast, sloshing some on his foot. "Dammit." He shook off his boot and walked back inside, wishing he could shake off the feeling left behind by the small movement of the curtain.

When he made it back into the bedroom, Clara had tucked Jeremiah under the sheets with only his right leg exposed. The nearly hairless limb reminded Cade of just how young the boy was.

"Took you long enough. Put the bucket here so I can get his foot in it." Clara pointed to the floor next to the bed, and Cade obeyed like a houseboy.

It would've been funny if he wasn't annoyed by his behavior.

She put the boy's long, skinny foot into the ice-cold water, and he woke up in a hurry. Jeremiah tried to lunge off the bed, but Clara held him down securely, which surprised the hell out of Cade. She was tiny enough to be half the boy's size, yet she was apparently solid muscle.

"Settle down, I've got you." Clara touched Jeremiah's

brow. "Go tell his pappy what happened." She didn't even look at Cade when she ordered him around.

"Who's his pappy?" Cade was happy to leave the tiny woman's domain, if only to stop jumping like a dog whenever she barked at him.

"What are you, the village idiot? Just find Sam and tell him Hiram's boy's been hurt." Clara dismissed him and Cade let her.

He left the house feeling as if he'd been through a twister and survived to tell about it. Meeting Clara the healer had been an experience, that was for sure.

Sabrina grew more concerned about Ellen as the minutes ticked by. She walked around the store peering out the windows, muttering to herself and shooting glances at Sabrina.

It was a little creepy, truth be told.

"Ellen, what are you doing?" Sabrina gave up trying to pretend she was still dusting.

"Watching him to make sure he doesn't come over to the store. I just saw him in the backyard at Clara's with a bucket." Ellen let the curtain drop. "He's just so dark, Brina."

The childhood nickname melted Sabrina's annoyance with her little sister. Ellen might be odd, but their sisterly love ran deep, and she'd always be in Sabrina's heart. The business five years ago with Eric was buried with him. She'd forgiven both of them for what had happened. They'd already been punished enough.

"Don't worry, Ellen. He's no threat to me." A lie, of course, because he already threatened her sleep, but something deep inside her knew there was much more between them than that. "I'm going to go check on Jeremiah."

Sabrina almost ran out of the store, sucking in a breath of fresh air. She wasn't sure if she wanted to see Cade or not, but she did know she had to get out. Ellen was in one of her moods, this one worse than many others, and sometimes Sabrina just had to escape.

She looked down the street toward the mill and saw a man in a wagon with a horse tied to the back riding toward the mill. *Cade.* A sigh burst from her throat at the sight, whether it be from relief or longing, she wasn't willing to think about it. Instead, she walked over to Clara's house and turned her gaze from the sight of the man who had found his way into her mind.

When Cade climbed down from the wagon at the mill, a big burly man with a reddish face and angry eyes ran from the mill, straight toward him, with fists raised.

The last thing Cade wanted was to show the townspeople just how skilled he was, but he had no choice. With a quick step and one right hook, the stranger hit the cold dirt with a thud.

"I don't have any quarrel with you, mister." Cade stepped back, hands raised. "But a man's got a right to defend himself."

Another man arrived, this one dressed in nicer

clothes, more than likely the owner of the lumbermill, Sam Fuller. "What the hell are you doing?" Sure enough, right behind him came the little imp who'd pestered him a week ago, Melissa, with her kinky hair and wild ways.

"Daddy, that's Mr. Brody. I saw the whole thing. Hiram ran outside with murder on his mind and so Mr. Brody had to defend himself." She turned a worshipful gaze on Cade.

Ah, fuck.

"Mr. Fuller, Cade Brody." He stuck out his right hand, which Sam promptly looked at like it was a pile of lizard shit. "I brought in Jeremiah to Clara Weathers with a broken foot. She sent me to tell Hiram his boy had been hurt. I ain't got a quarrel with this man, but he tried to pound me into the ground."

Cade's stomach jumped around like a pack of frogs. In between the flying turnip, the boy getting hurt, the tiny woman ordering him around, the giant trying to make him tiny and now the lumbermill owner and his apparently infatuated daughter, the day could not possibly get any worse.

Then Frenchie, that stinky mountain man, appeared behind Fuller with a grin on his furry face. Cade wanted to pound the little son of a bitch.

Sam frowned at Cade so hard, his brows met over his nose. "That'd be Hiram you just knocked into next week."

Well, Cade guessed the day could get worse. Next thing would be Melissa telling her daddy she wanted to marry him. A shudder snaked down his skin at the thought. He needed to get the hell out of Eustace and back to Livingston Valley where he could hide in peace.

"Hiram came out swinging. He had to expect me to swing back." Cade rubbed the back of his neck, trying to will away the craziness around him. His knuckles throbbed from the contact with the big man's jaw.

"He's twice your size, Mr. Brody, and you don't have a mark on you. Frenchie came running in the mill yapping about somebody hurting Jeremiah, riled up Hiram right good." Sam looked Cade over with a healthy dose of suspicion. "Just who are you?"

Frenchie snickered, a gleeful expression on his face. Cade reminded himself that he was a peaceful man, no matter what he'd just done to the big lumberjack or what he wanted to do to the odiferous tiny miner.

"Daddy, did you hear what he said? Jeremiah's got a broken foot and Clara's fixing him up. Don't you think we should be worried about him?" Melissa pulled at her father's large, unmoving arm. "Let's go make sure he's okay."

Melissa's cajoling broke the dangerous air between the men. Although Cade didn't want to be beholden to the girl, he tipped his hat at her as he backed away. "I'll just be taking my horse and leaving then."

Melissa winked, the little vixen. Cade really needed to stay away from town altogether. Perhaps he could get his ghost to come into town for supplies from now on.

Without a backward glance at the lumbermill and the strange folks in front of it, Cade turned to ride out of

Eustace.

Sabrina had been friends with Clara since they were children. Many of the girls in Eustace refused to be near Clara as though they thought whatever kept her short was contagious. Her mother had been the midwife and had taught everything she knew to Clara. Now she took care of everyone in Eustace, even if they treated her as an outsider.

Clara covered her hurt by being gruff with everyone. Sabrina never let the gruffness bother her and had somehow wormed her way into Clara's tight circle of friends. It was a small circle that included Sabrina, Antonio, Melissa Fuller and Ellen.

As she opened the door to the house, Sabrina called to her friend. "Clara, are you in the back?" The back bedroom was the unconventional examining room, where most of her patients were seen if they came to her house.

"Yep." Clara's voice floated through the house.

Sabrina made her way to the back room as fast as she could, concerned by the worry in Clara's voice. Within seconds, she was at her friend's side, alarmed at the waxy look of Jeremiah's skin. His right foot was immersed in a bucket, and his gaze roamed around the room as if he didn't know where he was.

"Can I help?" Although she wanted to ask how Jeremiah was, Sabrina knew better than to ask inane questions of her friend.

"Get some more well water and bathe his forehead.

He's starting to run a fever and I don't know why." Clara didn't mince words.

Sabrina made quick work of helping out, having a rag on Jeremiah's forehead within minutes. He relaxed as soon as the cool cloth touched his skin. She glanced at Clara.

"What happened to him?"

"Your Mr. Brody told me lumber fell on Jeremiah's foot so he wrapped it up tight and brought him into town. It's swollen like a melon, but lucky for him, the bandage kept it safe while they bounced their way into town on that old wagon of Sam's." Clara tsked loudly. "I told him he needed to replace the wheels on that thing months ago. I also told him Jeremiah was too small to be delivering wood on his own."

Sabrina had heard Clara's litany before but once she built up a head of steam, it was best to let her blow it all off. As she continued, Sabrina glanced out the window and saw Cade slowing down in front of Clara's. She wrestled with herself as to whether or not to go outside and talk to him since there was no reason to.

None of it mattered though because Sabrina found herself on her feet and murmuring to Clara that she'd be right back.

Once she stepped outside and he spotted her, Sabrina felt like an impulsive fool. The expression on his face told her everything she needed to know about Cade Brody's feelings for her. However, someone had raised him to be a gentleman, because he pulled the horse to a stop.

"Mr. Brody." Sabrina clasped her hands in front of her, the palms still damp from putting the cloth on Jeremiah's forehead.

"Mrs. Edmonds." He touched the brim of his black hat.

"Clara told me what happened. I just wanted to say thank you for helping Jeremiah." She sounded rushed and a bit out of breath.

He stared at her hard until she started to feel uncomfortable. "I believe you mean that."

Sabrina frowned. "What does that mean?"

"Not everyone in Eustace is glad to see me or thank me for helping the boy." He flexed his hand on the saddle horn. "Especially the boy's pa."

"Hiram? What did Hiram do?" She knew the man to be a bit of a blowhard, but he had no reason to be unfriendly to Cade, particularly if he'd helped Jeremiah.

"Tried to show me how hard his fists were." Cade's lips pinched together.

Sabrina couldn't have been more surprised or embarrassed by how he'd been treated by Eustace's townspeople. "I'm so sorry, Cade." She reached out and touched his knee, not realizing until too late that she shouldn't have done it.

A spark of something hot jumped between them. It traveled up her arm, then spread through her whole body. She'd only touched him once before and now she knew she shouldn't have ever touched him. She sucked in a gasp, which was echoed by Cade.

Sabrina opened her mouth but nothing came out, and for some reason, she couldn't pull her hand away. It seemed to be content to rest on his muscular, warm leg. Sweet heavens, he was even wearing the trousers she'd sold him.

The air between them grew heavy, and Sabrina's blood flew around her body as she heated between her legs. Cade was a handsome man, a sexy man. Although she'd seen many good-looking men, something about him struck a chord within Sabrina. It resonated strongly as pure need slammed into her.

"What's happening?" she whispered.

Cade's dark eyes looked even darker as his pupils dilated and his nostrils flared as if scenting Sabrina. "I don't know."

"Come into the store."

He shook his head even as he dismounted and secured the horse to the hitching post in front of the building. Sabrina trembled with the need to kiss him, touch him, absorb him. She hoped Ellen had taken herself upstairs for at least an hour, because Sabrina didn't think she'd be able to stop once she got started.

As soon as they stepped inside, Sabrina kept walking, leaving him to close and lock the door. At that point, she was possessed by hunger and only Cade could satisfy the craving.

Sabrina walked behind the curtain that hid her office. It was a small room, but it held a potbelly stove, a desk and chair. She didn't bother to light the lamp, the darkness felt soothing to her sizzling skin. One time, she and Eric—

She cut the thought off before it could completely invade her mind. This was not the time to think about anything, it was only time to feel.

Within seconds, Cade was there in the shadowy office behind her. His long, lean body pressed against her, and her entire body sighed with relief.

"What are we doing?"

Sabrina whipped around, and instead of answering his whispered question, she pulled his head down and kissed him. Oh Lord, his lips were as hard as she expected them to be. She used every meager trick she had to soften them until finally he relented and his arms wrapped around her. Sweet, long, openmouthed kisses followed. Sabrina could've kissed him for days on end. He had the most intoxicating, sensual lips she'd ever had the pleasure of experiencing.

His hands were busy roaming up and down her body, leaving goose bumps in their wake. He pulled her closer to him until she cradled his erection against her soft belly. Tingles spread out from the contact, heightening her already-burning arousal.

Sabrina clenched her eyes shut as the sensations almost overwhelmed her. It had been so long since she'd been intimate with a man, and this one engendered more feelings than she ever thought possible. Eric had been gentle, sweet and undemanding in their marriage bed.

Nothing prepared her for the onslaught of sensations

when she was in Cade's strong arms. She immersed herself in the absolute pleasure with more abandon than she'd known she had. Her nipples grew hard enough to ache for his touch, but since she still had her clothes on, she had to settle for pressing them against his chest.

Their kisses grew longer, hotter, deeper until Sabrina had trouble remembering her name. She needed more than just their mouths touching though, much more.

Cool air hit her legs as he raised her skirt, his large hands cupping her behind. Her heart raced with anticipation of what she was about to do. She'd never been so impulsive, so naughty in her life.

It felt good.

When Cade's finger found the slit in her drawers, she bit her lip to keep the scream in her throat. Sweet heavens, he slid back and forth in her wetness, teasing and tantalizing her swollen nub until she thought she'd bite right through her lip. He must have been unbuttoning his trousers as he pleasured her because the next thing she knew, his cock nudged at her entrance.

Five long years she'd been without a man, except in her dreams of course, and here she was about to have sex with a virtual stranger. Sabrina spread her legs a bit wider, never so ready for more.

As he pushed inside her, tingles raced through her. His cock stretched her long-unused channel, inciting a mixture of gratification and discomfort until all that was left was bliss. Oh how she'd dreamed of being with him, but the reality was much better than the fantasy.

"You're so fucking tight." He leaned forward and whispered in her ear. "Am I hurting you?" His voice sounded strained to the point of breaking, exactly how Sabrina felt waiting for him to move.

"No, please, I need..." She could hardly form a coherent thought as her body screamed for his.

"Yes, ma'am."

He pulled almost all the way out then slid back in, slow enough to send her to the brink of madness before withdrawing again. Sure, measured strokes left her panting, literally, for more. Her fingernails scrabbled at the desk for purchase so she could thrust back against him. She finally got hold of the side and top of the desk and met his stroke with one of her own.

"Faster," Sabrina managed to growl.

Cade, it seemed, didn't need to be told twice. She'd unleashed a beast and hung on for the ride of her life. He held her hips as he pumped in and out, faster, harder than she'd imagined. Delicious heat flowed between them as her body took everything he gave.

A crescendo built inside her, spiraling up along with her moans. She tried to be quiet, but couldn't stop herself. It had been so long since she'd felt pleasure, much less ecstasy, that she reacted like a woman freed from confinement—with abandon.

"Ah, God, Sabrina." His fingers dug into her skin through her drawers. "I can't hold on much longer."

The sound of harsh breathing filled the little room along with the heady scent of sex. She reveled in both, even as her body reached its peak, bucking against the desk as he plunged in deep, a low growl vibrating in his throat.

Sabrina felt like an animal with her mate, a bitch in heat who needed a good fuck, and oh, what a good one it was. As the waves of bliss faded from her body, he withdrew and pressed a cloth to her throbbing pussy.

"Take this." Cade stepped back after she took the cloth from him.

It took a few moments for her to catch her breath and be able to stand. He stared at her, a mere three feet away, his nostrils flaring as the scent of their mating permeated the air.

"I ain't gonna say I'm sorry."

"Good because I'd slap you if you did." She laid the cloth sideways in her drawers to keep it in place then fixed her skirt. God, her body still thrummed with an arousal not quite quenched by what they'd just done. Sabrina had a feeling she'd had only a taste of heaven and would need much more to be satisfied.

"I should go." He made no move to leave.

"Kiss me goodbye then."

Cade descended on her, snatching her up in his arms for a deep, penetrating kiss that shook her to her bones. His tongue swept through her mouth, dueling with hers in a dance she was coming to crave. He finally released her lips with an audible pop and stepped back, looking as shaken as she was.

Without another word, he tipped his hat and

disappeared through the curtain.

Sabrina pressed her hand to her mouth and took a shaky breath. She wasn't sure what had just happened, but she did know it wouldn't be the last time.

Chapter Five

Cade stumbled out of the store and took a moment to gather his fractured thoughts. Sabrina had surprised the hell out of him, and he had surprised himself. He certainly hadn't intended on having sex on her desk in the back office at the store. But damn if the experience didn't leave him as weak as a newborn baby.

His knees shook as he went down the steps toward his horse. The gelding bumped him with his great head as Cade reached for the reins. If he hadn't caught the hitching post, the cold ground would've likely broken his fall.

"What the hell is wrong with you, horse?" Cade grumbled as he regained his balance.

The horse responded by baring his teeth.

"Your *caballo* giving you trouble, *amigo*?" Antonio stepped up beside him, a big grin on his olive-toned face.

"More like a *diablo* than *caballo*." Cade glared at the offending equine.

"I heard about what happened at the mill." Antonio leaned against the front porch beam. "Hiram never could control his temper, part of the reason Elisabeth refused to marry him when she got pregnant with Jeremiah."

Cade's confusion blew away on the wind at the mention of the mill incident. "Well, I hope I never run into him again, temper or not." He'd tried to stay out of Eustace's business, but the town kept sucking him back in. "Who's Elisabeth?"

Dammit, he hadn't meant to ask but the question just popped out.

"My sister."

Surprise slammed into Cade. "Jeremiah is your nephew?"

"*Sí*, he is my nephew. My mother didn't want him to work at the saloon so she let him work for Sam instead." He shrugged. "Many folks in town look down on a bastard child, but Sam never treated him as anything other than a boy."

"So you think he's big enough to be driving a wagon around delivering wood?" Cade didn't want to admit what he'd been doing at the age of fourteen. His childhood was nothing less than a nightmare. With Antonio as an uncle and the rest of Eustace looking after him, Jeremiah couldn't possibly have been in the same position.

"His heart is big enough and he's a smart boy, knows his limits." Antonio gestured to Clara's small yellow house. "I just left him with Clara, and I wanted to catch you before you left to say thank you. She says he went into shock and if you hadn't brought him into town, he might've been in real trouble."

Antonio held out his hand and Cade shook it, a silly tremble of emotion making his voice vanish.

"Let me feed you a hot meal at least. I've got to move Mamá downstairs this afternoon so the saloon is closed until after she's settled. We can have tamales with my special blend of peppers, garlic, onion and brown sugar." Antonio's dark eyes appeared earnest and grateful.

Cade couldn't say no, even though he knew he should get the hell out of Eustace as fast as possible. Instead, he found himself nodding.

"Be glad to join you for dinner, and I'll help you with your *Mamá* too." He led his horse away from the store, away from the hot, incredible woman who'd just turned his world sideways with her passion and her heart.

Cade felt somewhat numb, as if he'd escaped from being himself. Too much emotion, physical happenings and intense up-close time with people was what threw him the most off-balance. He'd spent so much time amongst people but not with them, it was draining to remember the right thing to do or say. In his case, he was also usually recovering from doing or saying the wrong thing.

After they arrived at the saloon, Antonio showed him where to put his horse in the corral out back. The bay happily left him for hay and water and communing time with two mares. Cade had entirely forgotten to leave his horse by water while he'd been...visiting with Sabrina.

His body jumped at the intense memory flash of the softness of her skin. He beat it away with effort, intent on being normal in front of Antonio.

They walked through the back door straight into the kitchen. The delicious aroma of Mexican food reminded him he hadn't eaten since much earlier that day.

"God, that smells wonderful." Cade sucked in a lungful of the spicy scent.

Antonio chuckled. "I hope it's not burned. I left in a hurry but I did take the pan off the hot part of the stove. Please sit and I'll get some dinner for us."

Cade sat at the rough-hewn wooden table, strangely content again in the company of the soft-spoken man he wasn't ready to call friend. Antonio was one of the first people Cade had met who was comfortable with who he was and what he had. There was a kind of calm that existed around Antonio, one that Cade envied.

Apparently skilled in the kitchen, Antonio served up tamales for both of them in minutes, with hot steaming meat covered in the tastiest spices. Cade peeled the cornhusk back and bit into the hot concoction. His mouth exploded with flavor.

"Damn, if you were a woman, I'd marry you." Cade spoke around the mouthful of deliciousness.

"Thank God I'm not a woman." Antonio laughed.

They ate together, without the need for frivolous conversation. To Cade, it was the first relaxing moment he'd had in a while. The spicy Mexican tamales were the perfect way to bring him back from the razor's edge he'd been dancing on.

After they ate, Antonio left the dishes in the wooden

sink and put a top on the pan with the meaty filling.

"I've got to finish moving Mamá downstairs before dark. She can't get up and down the stairs anymore since she broke her hip, and I can't keep her out of the kitchen. So I finished the room behind it for her." Antonio gestured to the door to the saloon. "Help yourself to whatever you'd like to drink."

The raging whiskey demon that lay sleeping within Cade roared to life at the suggestion he could have whatever he'd like. Although he'd drunk water with his meal, he was thirsty again. He actually smacked his lips at the thought of the amber liquid. He knew better than to even step into the saloon in the condition he was in. God knows he'd probably never make it out on his own power.

"No, thanks for the offer though. I'll give you a hand with moving your *mamá* though. If you want the help."

Antonio smiled, a flash of white in his face. "Well I'm not about to say no."

They headed upstairs, Cade wondering what the hell had possessed him to volunteer to help. He didn't like families, especially mothers. They made him nervous, jumpy and downright uncomfortable. He expected no less of Mrs. Rodriguez.

Her room was at the top of a very steep staircase in the back of the saloon. The steps were well swept and smelled of pine oil. Antonio knocked and a murmured greeting came from within the room. He glanced at Cade. "Ready?"

Cade frowned and waved his hand forward. No need

to let the world know about his problems with people's mothers. Most folks had one they could rely on, but there were definitely exceptions to that rule. He followed Antonio into the room and was struck by the connection between the man and his mother.

She couldn't have been much taller than Clara, although Mrs. Rodriguez stooped over as many old ladies did. She had steel gray hair and eyes sharper than the knife currently residing in Cade's boot. After a minute of pure hell while she looked him over, he began to itch as if an army of ants marched up his spine.

What a fucking day.

"Mamá, this is the man I told you about, Cade Brody. He helped Jeremiah when he was hurt today."

Mrs. Rodriguez's stonelike expression melted at Antonio's words. "Ah, *bueno. Con mucho gusto, Señor Brody. Gracias por tu ayuda.*"

"*De nada,*" Cade answered in Spanish, unwilling to accept more than passing thanks for what he'd done. Truth be told, he had been annoyed the kid had hurt himself. Driving him into Eustace wasn't a heroic feat.

Without further ado, Cade and Antonio carried her dresser and bed downstairs, followed by the woman herself, who couldn't traverse the stairs alone. The last items left in the room were in a crate by the rocking chair—a cross, a lock of dark hair in a braid and a photograph of Antonio with a younger female woman. Cade assumed it was his dead sister, Elisabeth.

"That was my wife." Antonio appeared beside him,

startling the shit out of Cade.

Used to be no one could come within a hundred yards of Cade without him being aware of it. Now he didn't have enough sense to hear a big Mexican walking up a set of wooden stairs.

Cade finally registered Antonio's words. "Was your wife?"

"Caterina. The most beautiful girl you ever met, inside and out. She died giving birth to our daughter two years ago. I threw the picture away, but Mamá kept it." For the first time Cade saw something other than contentment in Antonio's face. Pure, significant grief came to the surface so quickly, Cade stepped away.

He could not possibly accept anyone else's sadness.

"I'm sorry." Inane words but he didn't know what else to say.

"*Gracias.* I miss her every day." Antonio tucked the picture back into the crate and walked out of the room, leaving Cade to carry the rocking chair.

He wondered if Antonio's father had made it for his young wife when their first child came along. She probably nursed them, rocked them and sang to her children as they grew. Like a normal mother would.

Cade almost slapped himself at the melancholy foolishness that ran through his head. With a mental kick in the ass, he picked up the chair and headed back downstairs.

After getting Mrs. Rodriguez settled in, Antonio walked Cade out to his horse. As he was saddling the contrary bay, Antonio gazed off into the sunset, a frown creasing his brow.

"I saw you come from the store earlier."

Cade froze for a split second, his heart thumping loudly. He resumed checking the cinch, wondering what Antonio was going to say next, hoping he wasn't going to stick his nose into Sabrina's business.

"Sabrina is a very good friend of mine. Her husband Eric had also been a friend. I look after her and she after me—we share a bond, she and I, as a spouse who has lost." Antonio turned his serious gaze on Cade. "I like you, but I love her as a sister. Don't hurt her."

Cade's breath came out in cloudy puffs in the crisp night air. He hadn't expected Antonio to speak of Sabrina, but now he half expected to be warned off. Instead, he was gently reminded that she had people who cared for her.

"I don't plan on doing anything with her," Cade lied through his teeth.

Antonio shook his head. "You can deny what you like, but I know what I see, and I know what a man looks like who has known the passion of a woman."

Cade hoped like hell his hot cheeks didn't mean he was blushing like an idiot. "I don't plan on hurting her."

"I accept your word as a friend." Antonio clapped him on the back.

Unable to answer, Cade just nodded, grateful the night air hid the confusion and pain in his eyes.

On the way back to Livingston Valley, Cade had many conversations with himself, none of which were pleasant. He was becoming too involved with people in Eustace, and he should not have given in to his passion for Sabrina. She didn't deserve a broken man like him, and he didn't need a woman in his life, at least not one he hadn't paid for.

By the time he made it home, exhaustion had thrown its blanket over him, and he had a hard time resisting its allure. He rode up to his cabin, grateful for the light of the moon illuminating his path. Next to the door was a bucket of water and some turnips.

Cade shook his head at the "ghost" who'd been haunting him, absurdly grateful he could tie off the damn horse next to the cabin and not worry about getting him to the lean-to.

He slid off the saddle like a puddle of mud and barely remembered tying off the reins to the door handle. Losing consciousness quickly, Cade stumbled inside and onto the bed, where darkness finally claimed him.

Sabrina sat on the window seat staring up at the moon, wondering if she'd done the right thing. Ellen would no doubt completely disapprove, as would Clara and many others. They didn't matter though, only her own opinion mattered, and she couldn't make up her mind.

The experience with Cade had been the most intense, sensual banquet she'd ever had in her life. Sweet heavens, she could still feel his hands on her body and his unique scent in her nose. He was so different from anyone she'd ever known. The man seemed to exist one second at a time, never thinking about anything other than the moment. Sabrina secretly thought it was because if he thought too much, he might feel something, and that way lay a dark path.

It was obvious he struggled with inner demons, real or imagined, and Sabrina respected his right to privacy. She really wanted to ask him what had happened to make him so incredibly sad that he'd give up on life altogether, on happiness, on anything. Seeing him with Antonio through the window gave her a peek into another side of him.

She wanted more, stupid woman that she was. Here was this stranger, a man who wouldn't, or couldn't, care about her, and she was obsessed with him. It had started before they became intimate, really from the first moment she'd seen him step into the store. Ellen was right, there was a dark cloud around him, but Sabrina wanted to blow the darkness away.

She'd risk a lot to even try. Cade could tell her to go to hell, or worse yet, shatter her heart. None of that seemed important though because taking a chance with him was the right thing to do. Eric had always accused her of bringing in strays, of trying to fix everything around her, but she couldn't help it. Cade was damaged and Sabrina had a feeling she was the potion to make him whole.

The morning sunshine pricked at Cade's eyes. He lay there wondering what day it was, where he was and how the hell he got there. The previous day's events blossomed in his mind and he remembered everything.

"Shit."

It had started simply enough with wood for a corral, and everything had spiraled out of control after that. Complete, utter chaos, inside and out.

He rose with a groan, his body protesting each move he made. After lighting a fire in the stove, he heated water to wash. Lye soap and lukewarm water woke him up in a hurry. The bite of cold reminded him that winter was just a breath away from arriving.

The smell of coffee bubbling soon filled the cabin and Cade contented himself with scorching hot cups of it accompanied by beef jerky that could've substituted for shoe leather or reins.

He stopped the coffee cup halfway to his mouth, remembering way too late that he'd left his horse outside the front door, still saddled, with only turnips and a bucket of water. No cowboy left his horse like that, ever. Although Cade tried not to like the horse, and the stupid creature made it easy, he was still responsible for keeping it safe, and he'd failed miserably.

Cade yanked on his boots and flung open the door. The horse was gone, leaving behind a bucket of frozen water and half-chewed turnips.

"Son of a bitch." He went back inside for his jacket, not at all happy about searching for the damn horse in the frosty morning.

When he rounded the corner of the cabin, he spotted the bay nicely tucked into the lean-to, unsaddled and contentedly munching on hay. Cade wasn't used to folks being kind to him for any reason, much less no reason at all.

His mysterious ghost must have taken care of the chores he was responsible for, and it irked him at the same time it touched him. Cade didn't want to be beholden to anyone, much less some white-haired ghost. However, he couldn't deny that he now owed the stranger for more than vegetables. The horse could have taken sick or even died in the cold night.

With a sigh worthy of any thespian, Cade cupped his hands around his mouth. "Thank you."

No response was forthcoming from the woods, not that he expected any. The ghost did what he pleased, when he pleased and Cade didn't want to dance to that particular tune anymore.

After inspecting the horse and finding no fault with the care of it—the damn fool had even curried it—Cade went back to the house grumbling to himself. There on the front step was a pile of fresh turnips. He cursed loudly, then did it again. How did this unknown entity keep getting the best of him? He was ten, maybe fifteen feet away and didn't even hear a blade of grass move, much less a person.

"Fine, I'll eat the damn turnips." He scooped them up and stomped inside, his disposition not improved by the early morning visit.

With some potatoes and beef jerky, Cade cut up the turnips to make a soup. He was certain it would taste terrifically awful, but figured he'd at least try to cook something for himself. The one skill—okay there was more than one but this was the most important—he hadn't learned in his life was how to cook. Living out of bordellos, hotels and saloons gave him a taste for other people's cooking, and the convenience of food already prepared was perfect for a man who drifted through life.

While the soup bubbled away on the stove, Cade sharpened his knife, the familiar task soothing his frazzled nerves. He'd come to New Mexico to find peace, a place to live as an unknown, and to escape. Unfortunately so far he'd not found any of those things, in fact, it had been the complete opposite.

A glimpse of a white face in the window made him almost drop the sharpening stone on his lap. He was being watched and that not only bothered the hell out of him, it made Cade angry. He'd told the stranger more than once to leave him be, yet the bastard refused to listen. Jeremiah's ghost was going to be led into a trap.

After the soup was done, Cade dipped a bowl into the pot, absurdly pleased by the fact it didn't burn or smell terrible. In fact, it smelled pretty damn good. He sat at the table with his soup and hesitantly brought a spoonful to his mouth, hoping he was still being watched.

The saltiness of the meat mixed with the potatoes and turnips made for a surprisingly good first meal on his own. Cade gobbled up a bowl before remembering what he was supposed to be doing—trapping his mysterious benefactor. After a second bowl of soup was in his stomach, he was ready to lay the trap.

As casually as possible, he put a bowl of soup with a spoon on the front step, then addressed the woods beyond the cabin.

"Okay, the turnips were good. I made some damn soup so you might as well have some since you contributed to it."

Cade shut the door, then with grim determination, squatted next to the door as quiet as death. It could have been five minutes or two hours until he heard the spoon on the tin bowl outside.

With no small amount of glee, he flung the door open.

"Gotcha, you little shit."

Crouched on the front step, Cade was speechless to find not a woman but a young *girl,* probably thirteen or fourteen. Shock rendered him paralyzed while she ran like the wind into the woods. What the hell was he going to do with a young female ghost?

The spilled soup on the ground reminded him that he'd not only scared her, but he'd spoiled the dinner she helped to provide.

Son of a bitch. Could he never do anything right?

✧

"I know what you did."

Sabrina glanced up from sorting the mail to find Clara scowling at her.

"Good afternoon to you too." She went back to the envelopes, certain she was not going to like what her diminutive friend had to say.

"Don't do that, Sabrina. I need to talk to you about what I saw." Clara walked around behind the counter, glancing around her to make sure no one was listening.

For certain, Sabrina did not want to get a tongue-lashing, but that was likely what was coming.

"I saw that man come in here with you, the sign read closed on the door for at least thirty minutes. Thirty minutes, Sabrina! What were you thinking? Did you even think at all?"

Sabrina set the mail down and took a deep breath, angry with herself for caring what others thought and annoyed with Clara for chastising her.

"First of all, I love you like a sister. However, that does not mean you can judge me or my actions. I am a grown woman, a widow with nothing in her life but a store and a future with no husband or children. If I choose to be with a man, it's my business." She started shaking as the words tumbled out, unsure if she was about to lose a friend or gain a slap.

Clara opened her mouth to speak, then closed it and shook her head. After a moment, she sighed. "That stranger is not a good man, and I'm worried about you."

Sabrina's anger deflated as quickly as it had come. "And I love you for being worried, but I think you're wrong. Cade is a good man who's had a hard life. I can respect that and not judge him for it."

She waited for Clara to agree or disagree, but she just patted Sabrina's hand with her small one. "Be careful. I'm not the only one who noticed the closed sign."

With that, Clara walked out of the store, leaving Sabrina with a fluttery stomach and a sense of dread. She knew what her friend had said without really saying it. Sam must know, which would explain the missed Sunday visit. Doubt jumped on her back along with a bit of guilt. Had she destroyed her relationships in town by simply being with a man? That was a crazy thought, but Eustace was such a small town, it was possible.

She finished sorting the mail and set to work tallying the receipts from the morning. It had been quite busy with lots of folks starting to stock up on supplies for the coming winter. Accounting was her least favorite chore, but it helped her forget about Clara's disappointment and her own need to see Cade again. It simmered within her with a firm hold.

"I hate you."

Sabrina looked over to find Melissa Fuller at the entrance to the store, her face flushed and fists clenched.

"Melissa, what's the—?"

"You stole my man right out from under my nose. I know what you did, you...you whore." Melissa swiped tears from her cheeks with angry slashes of her balled-up fists. "It wasn't enough that you had my father dancing to your music, you had to take my future husband too."

Sabrina was absolutely stunned, not only by the girl's venom but by her accusations too. Sam had been right, Melissa was weaving fantasies around Cade, and Sabrina's reality had destroyed them.

"Melissa, I think you might be confused about a few things. Do you want to come in and talk?" Sabrina wasn't about to admit to a fourteen-year-old girl that she'd had sex with a stranger in the back office of the store. It was not something any girl should aspire to do, but circumstances were much different for a widow and a woman than for an impressionable young lady.

"I don't ever want to talk to you again. I'm going to tell everyone what you did so no one will talk to you again either." Melissa slammed the door so hard, the bell almost fell off the top.

Sabrina threw her pencil at the floor, frustrated with everyone and everything. She stomped over to the stairs and called up to her sister. "I have to go out for a while, Ellen. You need to mind the store."

Amidst Ellen's protests, Sabrina took her wool coat and headed outside for a long walk. Perhaps the crisp air would help clear her thoughts and heal the hurts.

Chapter Six

It had been more than a week since he'd seen Sabrina, and Cade had had no idea how boring life was going to be in a secluded valley. Another Sunday morning dawned sunny and cold, bringing another day of complete and utter nothingness. He'd built the corral for the horse, taken walks and rides, hell he'd even cleaned the cabin somewhat. Now he had nothing to do but nothing.

Actually it was worse than nothing, he had too much time to think. It was a dangerous activity for Cade. Memories came and went and he battled each one. It hadn't occurred to him that he needed something to keep his hands busy so his mind didn't take over.

It seemed like such a good idea to hide away in a valley, but that was before he'd met the Malloys and the only friend he'd ever had, Brett. They'd shown him exactly what it meant to be loved unconditionally, to be accepted no matter what, and to have a family, a real family, not a dozen two-bit whores pretending to be motherly.

They'd spoiled him, that family from Wyoming, and damn them for doing it. Cade wanted to turn back time to Cheyenne where he'd been hired to kill Brett's brother

Trevor and his lady, Adelaide. Cade had made the choice to walk away from the money, the life of a gunslinger, and start again. Brett had given him that chance on a run-down ranch, and until Cade's past had caught up with his present, it had been the best time of his life.

God knows it was more than Cade had ever expected, and now he was stuck with the longing for what he couldn't have.

He'd checked the cabin inside and out, he'd read Shakespeare two dozen times already and could recite the book from memory. Unfortunately there were no other books, no paper to write on, and he'd only bought enough wood to build the damn corral. Cade was slowly losing his mind and he had to do something to stop it.

He didn't know what though. His mysterious young ghost hadn't shown up since the incident with the soup. He'd scoured the woods for any sign of her, but hadn't found even a stray branch, not that he'd know what to look for. Outdoors wasn't something he was familiar with. Oh, he could start a fire and maybe catch a rabbit, but he was no mountain man, nor a tracker.

So until his little ghost showed herself, he was stuck waiting, alone. Right about then, he would've welcomed her, hell, he would've welcomed anybody.

He started talking to himself that morning.

Soon he started answering back.

Cade walked to the nearby creek to wash his clothes, absurdly grateful he had laundry to do. The beauty of the valley wasn't lost on him. The bare trees sat amongst their green brethren, waiting for spring to come again and bring them to life.

"Soon you'll be writing poetry." Cade snorted at himself. "Then I'll take to the stage and sing."

"And here I was afraid you were lonely. Do you want me to come back later?" Antonio appeared in the morning sunshine on a beautiful black horse.

"Hell no. You're not a figment of my imaginations, are you?" Cade was never so happy to see another human being in his life.

"I don't think so." Antonio dismounted and looked around. "I've never been up here before. It's pretty nice."

"Yeah, if you want to die of boredom. Tell me you brought a deck of cards." Cade picked up his soggy laundry and threw it on a rock to be done later.

"Better than that. I brought cards and something to quench your thirst." Antonio held up a full bottle of whiskey.

Cade's stomach cramped at the sight of his nemesis, but what could he do? He wasn't about to send Antonio away. He'd been desperate for company, for anything to distract him from his self-induced misery.

Now it appeared his misery would be compounded by the temptation he dared not give into. They walked back to Cade's cabin side by side without talking. Antonio seemed to absorb the beauty of the valley and Cade let him. He was busy trying to figure out how to avoid drinking any booze.

He started shaking the closer they got to the cabin.

Cade put his hands in his pockets to hide his trembling foolishness. Jesus, he'd turned into a woman. Darkness came with whiskey, and Cade had avoided it for more than two months. He didn't want to fall back into the pit, into the blackness that had claimed days of his life, and worse, to the amber liquid that kept an iron claw stuck in his gut and controlled his actions, bringing him to his knees as no one and nothing ever had.

Cade was saved by the unlikeliest person—his ghost of the woods. There on the steps was a rabbit waiting to be skinned for dinner and of course, a handful of turnips.

"Did you leave your dinner to go wash your drawers?" Antonio laughed.

"No, I didn't. That's from the ghost of Livingston Valley."

Antonio whipped his head around and looked at Cade with disbelief. "The ghost? You mean Jeremiah's ghost? I didn't think it was real."

"Oh she's real all right." Cade picked up the rabbit by the ears.

"She? The ghost is a *mujer*?" Antonio's mouth dropped open.

"Not quite a woman. A young girl, no older than fourteen if that." Cade set the rabbit carcass on a rock and started skinning it. "She's a slippery little thing too, and a bit of a smartass."

Antonio peered at the woods. "Is she watching us now?"

"No doubt. She probably knows when I take a piss."

Cade wrinkled his nose at the slimy feel of the raw meat. He threw the skin on the ground and walked toward the cabin, Antonio still fascinated by the woods. "Be careful, she likes to throw turnips too."

"Who is she?" Antonio caught up to him and picked up the turnips.

"Probably some kid without parents." Cade almost choked on the words. He didn't feel comfortable using the word orphan. He doubted his wild child would ever feel sorry for herself or want to be pitied.

"And she lives in the woods?"

"Do I need to smack you?" Cade frowned at the other man. "Yes, she lives nearby somewhere. She brings me food and vegetables and takes care of my horse sometimes too."

"Sounds like she's already picked a new parent." Antonio's brows rose as he regarded Cade.

Cade threw the rabbit into the sink. "That's a load of horse shit. I am nobody's father, never will be, never wanted to be." The words came out of his mouth like fire, burning everything and everyone around him.

Antonio stepped back with his palms facing out. "I was joking, *amigo.*"

"Not funny." He plunged his hands into the bucket of water on the stove to get rid of the blood and the guilt. "I don't know what to do about her."

Antonio frowned. "You need to get her out of the woods and into a real home."

"Ha. I wouldn't know what a real home was if it jumped up and bit me." Cade got the cold shakes even thinking about bringing a child into his house. He wouldn't know the first thing about taking care of anyone, especially a teenage girl. Jesus, he could barely take care of himself.

"You can't leave her out in the woods." Antonio glanced out the window. "There's more than four-legged predators out there." He looked almost pained by the fact that the girl lived alone in the cold wilderness.

"I don't think there's anyone around to take care of her, either that or she has a lousy parent." Cade winced. He knew it didn't matter how long she'd been out there, winter was coming and no one, adult or child, could survive a New Mexico mountain winter without adequate shelter.

"Do you know who she is?" Antonio seemed desperate to help the child.

Cade was desperate to forget she existed. Unfortunately, the kid had other ideas.

"No, it's not my business."

Antonio threw the deck of cards on the table. "You don't care about anybody or anything, do you? I thought maybe there was something in there besides a cold hardass, but maybe I was wrong." He slammed his way out of the cabin, leaving Cade alone. Again.

"Come to Eustace," Antonio shouted to the trees, which was becoming a familiar occurrence in Livingston Valley. "This fool can't and won't help you."

It was only after Antonio ran away like the hounds of hell were chasing him that Cade remembered two things. First, that Antonio had lost his daughter in childbirth, and second, Cade had just chased away the only companionship he'd had in more than a week.

Life was always sweet in Cade's world, and it just kept getting sweeter.

Friday morning dawned with a steel gray sky. Sabrina stepped outside and took a deep breath of the frigid air. It smelled like snow, which confirmed what every person in town had said during the week while they stocked up. Snow was coming and soon. Sabrina rubbed her hands on her arms but didn't want to go inside just yet. It had been a difficult two weeks since she'd seen Cade.

Not only did she miss him, a feat she didn't think possible since she hardly knew the man, but her body missed him. Sabrina had trouble reconciling the way she felt with what her mind told her she should feel.

"Thinking about me?"

Sabrina whirled around to find Cade behind her, bundled up in a thick black wool coat with a red nose and one of the saddest expressions she'd ever seen in her life. Without a thought, she launched herself into his arms, and a feeling of pure rightness flooded her. His lips found hers, and then there was no thought at all.

Sweet heat blossomed and spread through her the

deeper the kiss went. Sabrina didn't know how long they'd been lost in each other's mouths, but it ended when something hard and painful hit her in the back. She broke free from the kiss and sucked in a breath, partly from fear and partly from pain.

Cade caught her before she fell, his hands firm beneath her shaking body. "What happened?"

"You whore!" Melissa stood behind Sabrina, her young face twisted in an expression of hate. "I knew you were lying to me. You took him."

"Melissa, I never meant to do anything to hurt you." Sabrina's throat closed up at the hurt racing through Melissa's eyes.

"I'm not a good man." Cade seemed to understand what was happening. "No one to set your cap for, girl."

"I didn't set my cap for you." Melissa threw another rock. It bounced off Cade's shoulder, but he didn't even try to duck. "You told me you loved me."

Cade's eyes widened at the accusation. "You'd best be careful what kind of accusations you throw around, little girl. I never said such a thing."

"You liar." She threw a bigger rock. This one sliced across Cade's cheek, leaving a bloody trail on his whiskered skin. "You told me you were going to marry me."

Cade wiped at the trickling blood on his face. "I'll never marry anyone, especially not a little girl."

"I'm not a little girl," Melissa screamed, her young face flushed by emotion and the cold, as tears ran from her eyes.

Sabrina stepped toward the hysterical girl. "Melissa, please, let me take you home."

"Don't touch me." Melissa threw one more rock, which hit Sabrina in the forehead, bringing her to her knees.

Cade cursed and stepped in front of her. "Get on home now, girl, before you really hurt someone."

"I hate you, both of you." Melissa ran toward the mill, the stillness of the morning broken by her sobs.

"Sweet Jesus." Sabrina dug at the cold ground beneath her fingers. She shook with about a thousand different emotions. She should have talked to Melissa after the incident with her in the store a week ago, at least have talked to Sam, but she hadn't.

Cade pulled her up by her elbow, his face as hard as granite. He bent down and brushed the dirt off the front of her dress. Sabrina still couldn't believe what had happened. Five minutes ago she'd been alone, and now she had Cade by her side and accusations of hate ringing in her ears.

"Can you tell me what the hell just happened?" Cade led her up the steps into the store.

"No, I'm as confused as you are. I knew Melissa had woven some dreams around you, but I never expected this." Sabrina closed her eyes and tears pricked her lids. "She's hurt and scared."

"Well, so are you." He marched her right to the counter. "Do you have a rag and some water to get cleaned up?"

"Um, yes, there's a washroom right near the stairs." She pointed the direction for him and leaned against the counter, grateful for the support.

Within moments, he returned with a basin and a rag, then proceeded to dip it in the water and clean her face. The last thing she expected was a gentle Cade, particularly after being accused of lying to and manipulating a young girl.

Yet he was as gentle as her mother used to be. Sabrina stared into his fathomless dark eyes and tried to see into his soul. He focused on his task until he must have been satisfied with his work. With one finger he touched her forehead on the spot where the rock had connected.

"You've got a bruise already."

"I bruise easily, always have." She took the rag from his hands and cleaned his face. He tried to pull away, but she took hold of his chin. "No, you'll let me."

A frown creased his brow, but he stayed put. Sabrina took care to clean him as gently as he had done for her. When she was done, she leaned her forehead against his, their breaths mingling.

"I think Melissa created a story she made into her own truth, but I believe you." It must have been the right thing to say because some of the shadows lifted from his eyes.

He straightened and kissed her once. "That makes one of you."

Sabrina managed a small smile. On shaky ground,

she knew she could either embrace what she felt for Cade or run from it. Life had given her a choice—she could either end the budding relationship with Cade, if that's what it was, or throw caution to the wind.

"Will you go to dinner with me at Wylie's tonight?"

Cade looked surprised by the invitation. He must have known as well as she did if he accompanied her to the only restaurant in Eustace for dinner, the townsfolk would know there was definitely something between them.

"Are you sure?"

There was no turning back if they went to dinner together. Sabrina understood that and embraced it. She'd talk to Melissa and Sam to clear up any misunderstanding as soon as possible. Regardless of what others thought, and how hard the backlash may be, she was ready to take a chance on something new. Some*one* new.

"Yes, I'm sure. Never been more sure of anything in my life." She kissed him hard.

"Then my answer is yes." When Cade smiled, a real smile for the first time since she'd known him, the bottom dropped out of her heart. He was beautiful, completely and utterly beautiful.

Sabrina slid a bit toward being in love with him.

They spent the rest of the morning in the store, cleaning and working side by side. Sabrina's sister came downstairs once, gave her a look of utter disappointment, then disappeared back upstairs again. The little blonde was pretty in her own way, but she stayed in the shadows each time he saw her. Perhaps she had her own secrets to hide from.

It was nearly time for dinner, for their date. Cade sat on a crate of peaches, watching Sabrina add up the accounts.

"I have a ghost haunting my cabin."

She stopped writing and looked up at him. "A ghost? Like Jeremiah's ghost?"

Cade shook his head. "So you've heard his stories, then? I'm not surprised. I didn't believe a word of them, of course. That boy is a walking work of fiction."

"He does like to tell a yarn, but he's been adamant about that ghost since Louie told him about it." She shook her head. "Have you seen it?"

"Sort of." Cade told Sabrina everything that had happened at the cabin. She listened intently as he spoke, asking questions here and there. He found himself telling her more than he intended to, even about Antonio.

"Antonio has a big heart, the biggest in town. He does all he can to help folks, especially children." She put a fist against her chest. "Caterina and the baby's death, it almost broke him."

Cade's conscience had woken with a vengeance and it forced him to think about what Antonio had said. Idiot that he was, Cade left food out for the wild child every day, yet she hadn't returned until that morning. The sight of the fresh turnips on his steps left his gut churning.

That's when he decided to come to Eustace and ask

Sabrina for help. He didn't know what possessed him, but he knew if he didn't help the girl, she really would become a ghost. If he did one good thing in his life, he'd help the wild child.

Sabrina tapped her chin with the pencil. "I think the girl might be Bernice Wilkinson. Her father died of consumption about a year ago at Clara's house. He'd been on his deathbed when he showed up on her doorstep. He died before we found out what happened to his daughter. She would be about thirteen or so."

"That sounds about right."

"I only saw her once or twice. Blonde hair, kind of shy." Sabrina stared off for a moment or two. "Oh, I remember now. She loves peppermint. Asked her papa at least five times if she could have some and he kept saying no."

Cade had given her soup, once, and then scared her off. Although he'd tried, she never did take any food from him. He wished he'd had some peppermints.

"I want to help her." The words were almost forced from his throat, but they came just the same. "Will you come back to the cabin with me?"

Sabrina stared hard into Cade's eyes, not answering for what seemed like an hour. "Yes."

A sharp pang of something he hadn't felt before hit his heart. "Thank you."

The incredible urge to kiss her overcame him so he stepped over to the counter, cupped her face and kissed her until he was dizzy. Hot, sweet kisses that went straight to his dick. His gaze strayed to the curtain to her office.

"I don't think we should do that again." She looked as pained as he felt. "At least not here."

A whoosh of relief made him weak-kneed. She'd said she'd come back to the cabin with him. He could hold onto the anticipation of having her alone. The very thought sent a shiver down his spine. Then his imagination took off and he lost track of everything but the thought of her round behind in his hands.

"It's just about dinnertime. I'm going to go get my coat." With a quick kiss to his lips, she headed for the stairs.

After she disappeared, Cade was grateful for a solitary moment. It saved him some embarrassment while he used his iron self-control to get rid of the steel bar in his trousers.

She came back downstairs a few minutes later with her sister in tow.

"You're courting darkness, Brina." Ellen speared him with a harsh glare. "The stranger will bring you nothing but pain."

"Ellen, please, don't start this again." Sabrina frowned at her sister. "You're being very impolite."

Ellen folded her arms in front of her stomach and continued her visual dislike of Cade. He didn't know what the issue was that set off the younger woman, but he didn't have the time or patience to figure it out. As he stepped toward Sabrina to help her with her coat, Ellen sucked in a breath and scurried back toward the stairs, into the light.

Cade saw her for the first time in full view. She had a jagged scar running from the corner of her eyebrow down her right cheek, ending at the edge of her chin. Someone had carved her up like a goddamn turkey. No wonder the girl hated men. His annoyance with her blew away as understanding replaced it.

"I won't hurt your sister."

"You already have," Ellen snapped.

"Ellen, stop it." Sabrina buttoned up her coat, shooting apologetic glances at Cade.

Cade walked toward Ellen until she was flat against the wall with nowhere to go. He reached out and touched her scar with one finger. "You know a woman is more than what she shows the world. If she doesn't show the world anything, then she'll never be anything more than a shadow."

Ellen's blue eyes widened and her mouth opened and closed without making a noise.

"You need to make a choice here, beautiful one, because the darkness you're cowering behind will bring *you* nothing but pain." Cade leaned forward and kissed her forehead softly. "Good day to you, Miss O'Neill."

Cade walked back to Sabrina and held out his arm. She looked perplexed by his actions, but only murmured goodbye to her sister as they stepped outside. He understood Ellen better than she expected. Shadows and pain were something he knew all too well.

He shook off the residual melancholy as they strolled arm in arm to Wylie's, the restaurant that sat on the bottom floor of the hotel in town. Sabrina nodded and said hello to a couple of people. Some folks were impolite enough to stare, others replied with greetings of their own.

Cade felt like an animal out for display at the zoo. If he hadn't wanted to be with Sabrina so bad, he'd have said to hell with it and gone back to Livingston Valley.

"I usually go to Wylie's for supper on Fridays, but since I won't be here later, I'm glad you're here now to accompany me." Sabrina smiled at him, the brilliance of it going straight to his gut.

He was in trouble and he knew it. After the snow hit, he'd be prevented from coming into town very often, saving him from his apparent obsession with Widow Edmonds.

They sat at a table by the window and ordered without incident. Cade wanted to get up and leave, but he didn't, probably because the most fascinating woman he'd ever met sat across the table from him.

She didn't seem to be afraid of anything or anybody. Not only that, but she wasn't constrained by what society thought. Cade had been surrounded by women the first thirteen years of his life, but not one of them even came close to being as lovely or amazing as Sabrina. During the meal, he found himself fascinated by the way she moved.

"I have to confess something." She glanced down, her thick lashes hiding her eyes. "I've dreamed of you since the moment we met."

Cade's fork stopped in mid-motion, his heart thumping erratically at her confession. "You've dreamed of me?"

"Yes, I did." She brought the fork to her mouth and licked off the gravy. It seemed Sabrina had decided on seduction without even touching him.

His body reacted as if she'd thrown a bottle of whiskey on a fire, blazing hot. It was a damn good thing she was going to his cabin with him or he'd walk around in pain for days.

When Sam Fuller appeared in the doorway of the restaurant, Cade's stomach dropped. Sam stomped over, his expression as hard as the fists by his side, then focused on Sabrina. "I need to talk to you."

Sabrina met Cade's gaze and the spell of sensuality she'd been weaving shattered.

"Please sit." She deliberately put her hand on Cade's, letting Sam know exactly what was going on. Her palm was as sweaty as his—she'd been just as affected by their sexual games.

Cade had the absurd urge to stick out his chest and crow like an idiot. "Mr. Fuller." He maintained a polite tone since the man hadn't punched him yet.

"I see felicitations are in order." Sam sat heavily, his expression never wavering. "You've chosen yourself a man."

Sabrina pinched her lips together. "Is that why you came to see me?"

"No, Frenchie came running over and told me Melissa had been throwing rocks." Sam glared at Cade. "I wanted to make sure you were all right, but I guess I needn't have worried."

"Melissa took her fantasies a bit further than we thought. She got angry with me because I was, ah, kissing Mr. Brody." She still had the feminine need to blush. "I'm afraid she took it really hard."

"I can understand that." Sam bowed his head and put his fists on the table.

Cade readied himself for a fight. He stupidly reached for the gun that hadn't sat on his hip for a damn month. When the hell was he going to stop doing that?

"I'm sorry, Sam." Sabrina's earnest apology earned her a slight softening of the big lumberjack's face.

"I guess I always thought you'd change your mind."

"Not after two years. I thought it had just become a habit with us."

He shrugged one shoulder. "I never expected..." Sam glared at Cade.

Cade resisted the urge to glare back. In fact, he made his expression as neutral as possible. The key to beating an opponent was to maintain control over everything, from his breathing to his sweat.

"Neither did I," Sabrina admitted. "But we have to go where our heart leads us, Sam."

Heart? Did she say heart?

"I'm sorry about what Melissa did." He gestured to the

mark on her forehead. "I should paddle her fanny for it."

"Please don't. She was hurt and angry. I'm sure she didn't mean to actually hit me."

Cade disagreed with Sabrina—Melissa meant to hit both of them. Folks who get hurt want to hurt others just as much, if not more. However, he kept his tongue and didn't interject into their conversation. Sabrina's comment about her heart still echoed through Cade's brain, and his heart.

Focus.

"I'm still sorry. Melissa needs a good whipping, and I aim to give it to her when I find her." He shook his head. "That girl needs a mother." His pointed look at Sabrina did not go unnoticed by Cade.

Son of a bitch. The man was trying to push Cade so far he'd lose control. He wouldn't give the bastard the satisfaction.

"I'll be on my way though." Sam stood, towering over them as if he could change Sabrina's mind by physical power alone. "Will I see you on Sunday?"

She swallowed hard and looked into Cade's face. "Probably not, Sam. I'm going to be helping Cade with a ghost."

"I don't know what the hell that means, but I'm no fool. I can feel the boot prints on my ass." Without another word, he walked away, leaving questions and disappointment over a ruined meal and mood.

"Let's go get my things." Sabrina paid for their meal, under Cade's protestations, and they left Wylie's more somber than when they'd arrived.

Cade escorted Sabrina back to the store with her arm tucked securely in his. The heat from his body chased away the chills left behind by Sam's visit. She'd seen the pain and anger in his eyes and knew she was the cause. Generally speaking, Sabrina made sure she didn't hurt anyone, but now it seemed she was going to hurt a lot of people.

"I'll stay out here." Cade stood by his horse, allowing her a few minutes to gather her things. "And bring some peppermint with you too, okay?"

Sabrina smiled and stepped into the store, certain Ellen would be as insistent as she had been earlier. Eileen Ryan was in the store with her two little girls. It was only a brief reprieve, but Sabrina was still glad to see them.

"Good day, Mrs. Ryan. I see you brought Lucy and Mary with you." She smiled at the girls, who hid behind their mother's brown skirt.

"Mrs. Edmonds." The redhead nodded at her. "I just needed some new needles. Your sister took good care of us."

"You're leaving already? How about a peppermint stick for each of the girls?" Sabrina took off her coat and walked quickly toward the counter and the glass jars of candy.

"Oh I don't know. I didn't bring enough."

The girls peeked out from behind their mother, watching Sabrina with wide blue eyes.

"No charge, Mrs. Ryan." Sabrina held out a peppermint for each of the girls. They looked up at their mother for permission. After Eileen nodded, the little redheaded imps took the candy with murmured thank yous.

After the Ryans left, Sabrina took a paper bag and filled it with peppermints, then went over to the girl's clothing and picked out a blue, serviceable dress and a pair of shoes. Sabrina walked around the store getting soap, a comb and some canned goods.

She was very aware of Ellen watching her, so was unsurprised when she finally broke the silence. "What are you doing?"

"I'm going to Mr. Brody's ranch. There's a girl living in the woods and he wants to help her. Don't worry, I'll tally up what I take and make sure it is paid for." Sabrina bundled everything in brown paper, tying the string tightly.

"What girl?" Ellen's anger had dissipated while Sabrina had been gone.

"I think it's Bernice Wilkerson, but I'm not sure. Remember her papa died at Clara's of consumption? Well, nobody knew what happened to his daughter so I think that's who Mr. Brody has seen in the woods."

"She's in the woods alone?"

"Apparently so. I'm going to try to help him so we can get her to town and a new home before the winter settles in." Stomach jumping, Sabrina made herself look at her sister. "I plan on staying up there for the weekend."

Ellen closed her eyes. "You know what people will say? They've just stopped talking about Eric and me."

Sabrina's heart lurched at the sudden memory. "I don't care what people say. Life is meant for the living, not the people who won't take a chance." Sabrina needed her sister to understand. "He's special, El, really special. I can feel it in here." She touched her hand to her heart. "On the outside might be a dark man who scares you, but inside he's someone very different than the face he shows the world."

"I don't think you should go." Ellen took Sabrina's hands in hers. "But I'm not going to try to stop you."

Sabrina could not have been more shocked. "You're not?"

"No, I'm not. I think you're right, it's your choice, not mine. I-I saw something in his eyes earlier, an ancient pain deep down that understood mine." She shook her head and sighed. "I still don't like him, but I'm not scared of him. And I know what it means to be in love and in pain."

Sabrina bit back a sob and hugged Ellen. "Thank you."

"You don't need to thank me." Ellen stepped back from the embrace. "Just promise me you'll be careful with your body and your heart. Don't make the same mistake I did."

"I promise." No matter what she promised, Sabrina had a feeling her heart was no longer in her keeping.

Chapter Seven

Sabrina walked out of the store with a lighter heart and a smile for Cade. He leaned against his horse's withers, hands tucked beneath his armpits. When he saw the traveling bag, a small grin played around his mouth.

"Do you have a horse?"

"Yes, it's at Antonio's." She handed him her bag. "We can ride down there and get her."

Cade nodded but didn't say anything, a frown creasing his brow. Sabrina remembered what he'd said about the falling out between him and Antonio. They'd have to talk to each other some time, so it might as well be sooner than later.

They rode in silence to the saloon, which was a few short minutes away by horse. After dismounting, he secured his horse to the post and they walked around back.

"What's your horse's name?" She could tell by his clenched jaw he was not happy about being there.

"Horse."

Sabrina laughed. "You need to give him a name. He's

a beauty."

"He's a pain in the ass." He opened the corral gate for her.

Sabrina smiled as she spotted her beautiful mare, a palomino who had been a gift from Eric on their wedding day. He loved to ride and always took the time to do so on Sunday afternoons with her. The memories were now sweet companions rather than painful visitors.

The mare trotted right over to her, nudging Sabrina's shoulder with her nose. "This is Felicidad."

"Pretty horse." Cade ran his hand along the mare's neck.

"I don't ride her as much as I'd like to. I'm selfishly glad I can today." She headed for the tack room. "My saddle is in here."

Antonio appeared in the doorway, a smile on his face. "Sabrina, *amiga*, it is good to see you." He glanced behind her to see Cade standing in the corral, and his expression hardened.

"You too, Antonio. I've come to get Felicidad. I'm, well, going to Livingston Valley." She suddenly felt her cheeks heat beneath her friend's scrutiny.

"Are you sure you want to do that?" Antonio kept his brown eyes pinned on her. "You could be making a big mistake, *un error grave*."

"I appreciate your worry, but I'll be okay." She stepped past him and into the tack room. By the time she emerged with the blanket, Antonio and Cade were toe to toe.

"I thought better of you, so did *Mamá*," Antonio was saying. "I can't allow you to take her."

"You won't allow me?" Cade snorted. "I'm not going to take her. Sabrina made her own choice."

"I am still here, you know." She walked to the horse, more than irked by the men talking about her as if she wasn't even there. After settling the blanket on Felicidad, she went back for the saddle while the two men faced off like bantam roosters.

Neither one of them even offered to help her. They just kept sniping at each other as she saddled the mare and secured the bit in her mouth. By the time she'd strapped her bag and the paper-wrapped package to the saddle, they were still at it.

"For Pete's sake, you two. Stop it, I order you." Sabrina yanked on their arms, pulling them apart. "I make my own decisions, and I do what *I* want to do. Antonio, Cade asked for my help with the girl in the woods. It was my idea to stay with him for the weekend."

Antonio's mouth fell open. "You what?"

"You heard me, now go take care of your saloon. Friday night is your busiest. Don't worry about me." She pushed at his shoulder. "I am a *mujer* not a *niña*."

"I don't like it." Antonio scowled at Cade.

"I think she's already told you to mind your business."

"I'm leaving." Sabrina led Felicidad out of the corral, knocking both men aside. She was annoyed with the whole situation, as if Antonio had any right to judge her.

Cade fell in step beside her until they reached the street. He didn't apologize and she honestly didn't expect him to. He'd only been reacting to Antonio's hostility, or perhaps it was vice versa. It didn't matter. Sabrina had made the choice to go to Livingston Valley with Cade and that was that.

"Sabrina, wait." Antonio ran out from behind the saloon and grabbed hold of the mare's reins. "I'm sorry, *amiga. Lo siento.*"

"It's okay, I understand. Cade told me what happened at the cabin." She patted his hand. "Your heart is just too big for your body."

Antonio smiled then turned his gaze to Cade. "Take care of her. She's *muy especial.*"

"*Sí, amigo, yo comprendo.*" Cade stuck out his hand. After a moment's hesitation, Antonio shook it.

"There, now that you've kissed and made up, we can go." She smiled at the frown on the men's faces, then a laugh bubbled up her throat.

It felt marvelous to ride away with Cade, his warm, strong presence comfortable by her side.

Cade didn't know how to feel after Sabrina had knocked him sideways again. He hadn't expected her to say yes to helping him, much less agree to come back to the cabin with him. Yet there she was riding beside him on her horse, ridiculously named "Happiness" in Spanish.

His body still thrummed with the sensual tension built up during dinner. Although Sam and Antonio had done their best to disrupt the energy between Sabrina and Cade, it was still there. He'd been fantasizing about being intimate with Sabrina again and it was about to happen.

When they rode into the valley, tiny flakes of snow began to fall, clinging to the horses' manes. A see-through blanket of white coated the roof of the small log house.

Sabrina gasped. "It's beautiful, Cade."

He had to agree with her. It looked so peaceful and welcoming, he felt like he was coming home. The feeling surprised him immensely.

"Yeah, it is, isn't it?" He led her to the corral and took care of the horses while she went in the cabin.

Inside, he found she'd started a fire in the fireplace and the potbelly stove. A half dozen turnips sat on the table as she stood next to the flames.

"Were they on the front step?" He gestured to the table.

"Yes, I figured they were from Bernice or whoever she is." Sabrina rubbed her hands on her skirt. He didn't know whether she was nervous or cold.

"Thanks for lighting the fire." He sounded like a complete idiot.

"And thank you for taking care of Felicidad." She pointed to the window. "Is it still snowing?"

"Yep, it is." Cade slipped off his coat and hung it up on a hook beside the door, startled to see her blue coat hanging there already. He swallowed hard, nervous with a woman for the first time in his life.

What made this so special? What made Sabrina so special? He didn't have answers to the questions running around his brain. He turned back to face her, realizing she looked as awkward as he felt.

"I've never spent the night with a woman," he blurted.

Even as he inwardly cursed his runaway tongue, her eyes widened. "Are you saying you're, um, inexperienced?"

"No, I forgot how to use my mouth and my brain at the same time, I guess." He took a deep breath. "Until you, I've never been with a woman I haven't paid for and spent about an hour with."

Sabrina's face registered surprise. "I don't know what to say to that."

"I'm sorry I said anything." Cade stomped over to the fireplace, sure his stupidity knew no bounds. The last thing he expected was to feel her hands touching his back.

"My marriage wasn't a love match. Eric and I were...friends and lovers. We found pleasure in each other's arms but it was only that, never deeper. He actually loved someone else who was promised to another." She pressed her forehead against the back of his neck. "Ever since we were together last I've thought of nothing but being with you again. I'm glad I'm your first."

Cade closed his eyes against the unfamiliar emotions skipping through his heart. He'd never had a woman be glad to be with him, particularly a well-bred, smart one who could have her pick of the litter. It left him with a peculiar sensation in his stomach, one that echoed through him like vibrations from a big drum.

He turned around and faced her, unsure of what he'd see in her blue eyes. "Tell me now to take you back to town or you'll be staying the night with me."

"Or perhaps two nights." A sexy grin lit her face as she wrapped her arms around his neck.

Cade shook with the need to snatch her off her feet and bury himself so deep inside, they wouldn't know where one ended and the other began. He wanted, he needed so much. If he opened the door to his heart much further, he might not be able to get it closed again. It had felt like a good idea when he asked Sabrina to come to the cabin with him. Now he wasn't so sure.

There was much more on the line than simple sex, although with her it was definitely not simple. His body reacted to just being within touching distance, so it was hard as steel the second she laid hands on him. This wasn't a quick fuck in the back of the store, it was a weekend alone together.

Her reputation would be in tatters, and folks in Eustace would give both of them the cold shoulder. Sam Fuller might knock his head into next week or maybe throw him under that three-foot saw blade in the mill.

She must have seen something in his eyes because her expression hardened. "I never took you for being yellow, Cade Brody."

The door within him burst open and everything poured out as if a dam had broken. He cupped her face and kissed her hard, yanking her close to him, feeling her body heat against his. Yes, yes, *yes*. That was exactly what he both wanted and needed.

Sabrina.

His skin sizzled with the energy caused by the mere fact that he held her in his arms. He backed her toward the pitiful excuse for a bed, intent on proving to her that her choice was the right one. Sabrina would know pleasure from him that night, more than she could dream of. After all, he'd learned from the best.

When they reached the bed, he scooped her up in his arms and set her gently on top of the blanket. The fire and their heat had warmed the little cabin up to sweltering, or perhaps it was just him that was overheated. Sabrina lay back on her elbows and crossed her legs at the ankle.

"Now what?"

"Now I show you how to give and receive." He started with her boots, the serviceable kind most women wore during the colder months. They protected against mud, snow and whatever else they happened to step in. Cade unlaced them and slid them off, followed by her stockings. She had beautiful, long legs, reminding Cade of a colt's in their sleekness.

He ran his hands up her calves, kissing the skin as he exposed it. Fortunately his thumbs hooked the bottom of her dress and hiked it up as he progressed, giving him a banquet upon which to feast. He lapped behind her knee, earning a kittenish moan. His body throbbed with the need to spread those long legs and plunge in deep, and he barely controlled the urge. Something inside him insisted he absolutely had to go slow or risk more than a quick fuck.

Her drawers were plain white cotton. A woman like Sabrina needed prettier underthings and he made a note to himself to make sure she got them. As she shimmied off her drawers, the scent of her arousal tickled his nose. He kissed and caressed his way up her glorious thighs, spreading her legs as he went. She didn't fight him or even say a word, she just watched wide-eyed.

Her dark curls beckoned him, daring him to take a sip of the nectar he was sure to find. However, he didn't want to scare her off.

"I'm going to touch you on your pussy. If you don't like it, tell me."

She swallowed hard at his frankness, but nodded her assent.

"You smell good." Cade leaned forward and breathed in her essence. Sabrina was a passionate woman, one of the most naturally passionate women he'd ever had the privilege of knowing.

He tasted her with one small swipe of his tongue, and a shudder of longing wracked him from head to foot. When she made no protest, he licked her from top to bottom, savoring the musky flavor. As he nibbled on her nubbin of pleasure, she ground her heels into the mattress.

"Sweet Jesus," she breathed.

"Not quite." He spread her nether lips wide, licking

and sucking while his thumb slid in and out from her tight, hot channel. She writhed beneath him, never breaking contact between them. Cade continued his sensual assault, even as his own body screamed for hers.

"Oh God, Cade, it feels too good. I'm going to, going to, ahhhhhhh." Her hips lifted off the mattress as he lapped at her surrender, absorbing every drop of her orgasm until she lay back on the bed in a boneless heap.

"Like it?" He held up his thumb. "You are like the nectar of the gods." As he licked her taste from his skin, her eyes widened, watching his every move.

Cade didn't know what possessed him, but he held his thumb by her lips, and her little pink tongue darted out to taste herself. His dick jumped when she did it again. She was a combination of natural sex and sweet abandon, all his for the taking.

"Undress." Her gaze raked him up and down, coming to rest on his burgeoning trousers. "Before you hurt yourself."

Cade choked out a laugh. "Too late."

She sat up and released her hair from its braid. The long brown strands cascaded like warm molasses ready for his touch. He couldn't resist the urge to touch it, to feel its silky texture on his fingers, its cool waves raising goose bumps on his arms.

"I can't wait to feel this on me when we make love." He didn't know where the words came from. He'd never made love in his life, nor had he expected to. He opened his mouth and suddenly his intentions didn't mean shit.

When they came together, they'd be making love.

"Then you'd best hurry in getting those clothes off." She grinned from the bed, looking like an experienced vixen.

Cade almost fell on his head yanking his trousers off, but within seconds he was naked and sliding into the narrow bed with her. When Sabrina's supple body finally pressed up against his, he groaned with the sweet pleasure of it.

"Oh God, you feel good." He pushed his hard cock into her soft belly, eager for more but trying to enjoy the sensation at the same time.

"You feel hard." She chuckled against his neck, then bit him gently. "Please, Cade, give me more."

He was afraid that after he got started he wouldn't give her more than five minutes, but he couldn't wait any longer. She lifted her knee, and he positioned himself at her moist entrance. Cade pressed his forehead against hers. Their breaths mingled and as he breathed her in, he entered her slowly.

Bliss, absolute bliss enveloped him, a sensation he'd never experienced before or dared hope to. His breath caught in his throat and he forced himself to swallow. After he got a smidge of air back in his lungs, he could move.

Sweet heat grew with his thrusts, spreading through him. His mouth found hers and they fused together, their tongues mimicking what the lower half of their bodies did. He plucked at her nipple, teasing the tender bud into diamond hardness.

"God, Cade, it feels amazing."

He managed a strangled chuckle. "I think I might have died and gone to heaven."

She nipped at his neck, sucking and licking at the skin. "Mm, we'll have to do this again later."

Just the thought of being with her again made his dick harder. He couldn't hold on much longer, and he wanted to bring her with him. Something inside him insisted on it. He abandoned her plump breast to pull up her knee, exposing an even more wonderful treasure. She gasped and tugged at his shoulder.

Cade held onto his sanity by a slim thread. He dipped his finger down to rub her nubbin of pleasure while his strokes grew deeper and faster. As the tingling in his balls signaled his release, he captured her mouth. Her hot channel tightened around him, drawing him into a spiral of ecstasy that washed over, through and around him.

He tried to shout her name, but nothing came out but a groan. Cade plunged into her, riding the wave of the most powerful moment he'd ever had. Ragged breathing and the crackling from the fireplace were the only sounds in the room.

Sabrina traced his jaw with her finger. He pressed her palm into his cheek, reveling in the softness of her skin and the connection between them. Cade knew he was in trouble, deep trouble with Sabrina. He was falling hard and fast for the woman in his arms.

The morning dawned gray and bleak, exactly the mood that struck Cade when he opened his eyes. What the hell had he been thinking to bring Sabrina alone to his cabin? And why the hell had she agreed? She lay beside him on the narrow bed, her soft breath warming his cool skin.

Jesus, he was in a whole mountain of shit.

As quietly as he could, he eased out from beside her and yanked on his clothes in the frigid air. After stoking the embers in the fireplace and the potbelly stove, he pulled on his boots and went outside in search of some sanity.

Small snowflakes fell from the sky, nothing heavy yet, but it was definitely starting to accumulate on the ground. The air had the bite of a storm, if he was any judge. No doubt it would last the day. The question was, would he?

He stomped over to the woodpile, which was dwindling fast. What he ought to do is put Sabrina's butt on her horse and take her back to Eustace immediately. As far as anyone would know, she came out to help him with the wild child and returned to her bed unharmed.

Cade snorted and contemplated hitting himself on the head with one of the logs. Perhaps the hard wood could make a dent in his pitiful brain. He picked up an armful and turned to head back to the cabin. A figure stood at the corner of the house, and it was way too short to be

Sabrina.

"Bernice?" He stepped toward her and she disappeared in a flash.

Cade dropped the wood and sprinted for the front of the cabin, nearly tripping on the logs as they tumbled on the ground. By the time he made it to the front door, she was gone. That damn kid was leading him in circles and he was tired of it. Sick and damn tired. He needed to get her sorry butt out of the woods and into town.

"What are you doing?"

Cade whirled around into a crouch, his hand reaching for a gun. If he'd had one, Sabrina would be dead. She stared at him with wide eyes, sporting tousled hair and his blanket. No doubt Sabrina's extremely sharp brain already concluded he was no miner or mountain man.

"Don't sneak up on me like that," he snapped as he straightened up.

Her bewildered expression now added hurt to it. Wonderful. Maybe he could find a few puppies to kick too.

"Sorry, I just don't like people to come up behind me. Old habits." He ignored any feelings of guilt that tried to creep up and headed for the fallen logs instead.

Sabrina didn't go back into the cabin nor did she make any move toward him. Cade was aware of every second she stared at him. It felt like sharp sticks poking his back. When he picked up all the fallen wood, he turned back to the cabin.

"Who are you?"

He hoped she wouldn't ask, and the question hit him hard. "Cade Brody."

"The way you say your name tells me it hasn't been on your tongue long. Don't treat me like a fool. I know there's a secret hiding behind those dark eyes of yours and I'm guessing it has something to do with the phantom guns you reached for." She jumped in front of the doorway, blocking his path. "I'm going to ask you one more time, who are you?"

"I'm nobody, a dead man who wants nothing but to be left alone." He gritted his teeth, determined not to yell at her anymore and trying to keep his secrets to himself.

"You want me to leave?" Her gaze was shuttered, hidden behind the cloud of dark hair.

"That's not what I said." Cade wanted to turn tail and get the hell out of there himself. The day had started out worse than he imagined.

Of course he could still feel her beneath him, the softness of her skin, the swipe of her tongue on his neck. Hell, he was arguing with her and about to make a tent in his pants just thinking about her.

"You said you wanted to be left alone."

"I meant I want folks to just accept that I'm not social-like or friendly. I came here to be alone." He tripped over his own words, unsure of what exactly he was trying to say.

"For a man who wants to be left alone, you sure do spend a lot of time in town. Where were you before you came to New Mexico?" She was like a stubborn mule.

Cade was through being polite so he pushed past her and into the cabin, Sabrina right on his heels. "Nowhere. I was born a month ago."

She took his arm. "Why can't you trust me?"

"I only trust but a few people in this world and none of them are you." It sounded so harsh, but he needed for Sabrina to let the conversation go. That way was nothing but trouble for both of them.

Cade dumped the wood on the ground, waiting for the firestorm to commence. She'd either accept what he said or continue dogging him. Hopefully she'd choose the former and do both of them a favor.

"I saw the girl." He gestured toward the door, annoyed to see a tremble in his hand.

"When?" Sabrina sounded business-like, no longer the sultry siren of the night before. By telling her he didn't trust her, he'd thrown their closeness back in her face like she was nothing but a two-bit harlot.

Cade hated himself at that moment. It took every smidge of his self-control not to simply ride away and disappear again.

"Just before you came out. She was standing in front of the cabin. Little bit of a thing too, not much bigger than Clara." Cade's voice was thick with what he figured were emotions, but he swallowed them down.

"Then let me get dressed so we can go find her." Sabrina headed for the fallen clothes.

Cade listened to the rustle of the fabric and his imagination took the low road, thinking of how she looked without all the geegaws women put on. She was, to be blunt, the sexiest woman he'd ever laid eyes on, and he'd just intentionally hurt her. He knew he was a bastard, had hurt many people throughout his life, but treating Sabrina so badly stung, a lot. She didn't deserve the shit he gave her, and he hoped she would learn a lesson and move on.

It was either that or risk more than getting hurt. Cade wasn't about to let it happen. He was meant to be alone and that was that.

"All right, Cade, let's go." She was already walking out the door, braiding her hair with crisp movements. Good, she needed to be angry.

He followed her out the door, sure he'd never felt so bad in his life. What was it about Sabrina that made him feel? He didn't want to feel anything, much less guilt, remorse and whatever the hell else ran around inside him. The snowflakes landed on his face, icy kisses to go with his cold, black heart.

"Look, there was enough snow on the ground for her tracks to stick." Sabrina pointed to small indentations in the brown grass. Hell, Cade hadn't even seen them much less picked them out as the girl's tracks.

Good thing he didn't try to work as a tracker.

"Can you follow them?" He peered toward the woods, certain the little shit was watching them and laughing.

"Yes, I can. I learned how to hunt and track when I was younger." She was just full of surprises.

"So you can handle a gun too?"

She glared at him over her shoulder, her blue gaze colder than the snow on his face. "Don't doubt it."

Cade should have kept his mouth shut, should have let the conversation end right there. He didn't.

"Who taught a woman how to hunt and track?" He knew the answer before he asked, yet the question popped out of his mouth anyway.

"If I wasn't so angry with you for being so stupid, I might slap you." She stopped to look at a broken twig and suspicious moss on a rock. "It just so happens my husband was an avid hunter. He taught me...a lot."

The implication couldn't have been any clearer if she'd kicked him in the balls. Jesus, was he really that stupid? Cade clenched his fists, nails digging into the skin as Sabrina verbally smacked him around.

"She's in the trees." Sabrina met his gaze. "Don't look up." She rolled her eyes as he instinctively raised his head.

"Why the hell not?" His head spun from the changes in subject. The woman was talking in circles.

"So she doesn't know we've figured out where her hiding place is." Sabrina spoke as if Cade were a two-year-old child.

"Fine then. Now what?" He folded his arms across his chest, annoyed, aroused and confused.

"We lure her down." She reached into her coat pocket and pulled out a paper sack. He knew what it was even before the familiar white and red stripes appeared in her hand. "She used to like peppermints. I'm hoping she still does."

"I like peppermints, but you didn't give me any even though I asked you to get them." Now he was starting to sound like a two-year-old child.

"Bernice?" Sabrina ignored him and meandered into the pine trees, the peppermints clearly visible in her hand. "It's Mrs. Edmonds. Do you remember me?"

Mrs. Edmonds. Cade snorted. Sabrina glared at him again.

"Could you act like an adult for five minutes?" she snapped.

Cade mimicked her under his breath, but then stopped pouting. What the hell was wrong with him? He'd woken up determined to be an adult and send Sabrina back to Eustace. Instead, he was in the woods, *again*, chasing the wild child, *again*. He didn't care about Bernice, or whatever her name was. He didn't care about anyone really, especially himself.

Yet he kept walking along behind the woman who'd spun him in circles, in search of the girl who'd driven him crazy.

If it wasn't so pitiful, he'd probably laugh.

"You know, I think a man is entitled to his secrets, but once he's been between a woman's legs, she's entitled to hear them." Sabrina did nothing but surprise him, constantly.

"Why don't you tell me what you really think?" Cade had the urge to spank her.

She laughed, a husky chuckle that sent a shiver up his spine, as she ignored his anger completely. Sabrina was skilled at many things, not the least of which was keeping him on the edge of insanity.

"Don't ever expect me to feed you a spoonful of sugar, Cade." She stopped at a particularly big pine.

"What are—?" he started to say.

She shushed him and made a chopping sound with her hand. Cade opened his mouth to tell her not to treat him like a child anymore when a small shadow dropped out of the tree. Good thing his instincts were still razor sharp. He ran after her, so close now he could see it was a girl, one who had kept him hopping for weeks. No longer.

Within a minute, he'd caught up to the black-clad girl and tackled her. Fortunately the pine needles on the ground cushioned them as they fell. She tried to scramble away but Cade was twice as big. What he didn't expect was Sabrina to smack him on the back of the head.

"Get off her, you big oaf. You're going to hurt her."

The girl beneath him struggled like a wildcat.

"If I let her up, she's going to run." He grunted when one of her heels connected with his ass.

"Bernice, it's okay. We're not going to hurt you. Mr. Brody is going to let you go." Sabrina yanked on his hair, bringing tears to his eyes.

Cade cursed and rolled on his back, just missing a hard-as-nails kick by the little wild thing on the ground. Between the two of them he was surprised he wasn't unconscious and drooling yet.

As soon as she was free, the girl stood up swinging, and her hard little fist connected with Cade's cheek. He took hold of her arm, stopping the second hit.

"Let me go or I'll pound you." Her high-pitched threat would have been funny if his face hadn't been throbbing.

"Stop it, both of you." Sabrina, to his ever-loving surprise, grabbed hold of the girl by the collar and had her under control in seconds. "We are here to help you, not harm you." She frowned at Cade. "And you, this isn't a saloon where you can start a fight with anyone who makes you angry."

"I didn't start it." Cade stood up and dusted off the dirt and pine needles from his trousers. "She started it a long time ago." He got the first thorough look at the girl who'd been plaguing him.

Bernice was not what he expected. Honestly, he'd thought she'd be a dirty, cross-eyed waif with buck teeth and critters living on her skin. Whoever her crazy pa was, he was lucky enough to make a child beautiful enough to hurt Cade's eyes. She had moonlight-colored hair, the lightest it could be without actually being white. Her eyes were the same shade as the moss on the rock Sabrina had been looking it, a deep, rich green. A heart-shaped face and skin the color of cream all came together to form trouble with a capital T.

No wonder the girl hid out in the woods. Every man in town over the age of sixteen would be after her like a hound scenting a bitch. Jesus, he'd never been so shocked by someone before.

"What are you staring at, fool?" The spell was broken when the girl opened her bow-shaped lips.

"A little shit who thought it was funny to throw turnips at me and scare folks." He pointed a finger at her. "I should paddle your ass."

She stuck her little chin in the air. "Just you go ahead and try it, gunslinger."

Cade's stomach dropped to his knees. "What did you call me?"

"I ain't as dumb as I look. I know what a gunslinger looks like and acts like. You are a gunslinger." She glanced at Sabrina, then at the peppermints still in the woman's hand. "I remember you. You work at the store in Eustace."

Sabrina held out the peppermints with a smile. "Yes, I sure do."

After the girl snatched the peppermints, she slowly backed away from both of them. Cade was trying to figure out how to answer the girl's accusations. Bernice wasn't even a woman yet and already well on her way to being a manipulative female.

"You've caused a lot of trouble." He wanted to curse until he ran out of words, but what came out of his mouth was pitiful.

Bernice ignored him as she munched on a peppermint. "What do you want with me?" She directed the question to Sabrina.

"We're worried about you surviving the winter out here by yourself."

142

"My pa's coming back." The tone of the girl's voice suggested even she didn't believe it.

"Honey, your pa passed on a while ago. We tried to find you after it happened, but we couldn't." Sabrina looked so empathetic, even Cade felt it.

Bernice shook her head. "He said he'd be back."

"Come with me to town and visit his grave. Then we can talk about where you want to live." Sabrina put her hand on the girl's shoulder, which only proved to demonstrate the enormous height difference between them.

"I don't want to go to town. The men are mean and stupid." She cast a baleful glance at Cade.

"Don't you lump me in with all the asses in town." He crossed his arms on his chest. "From what I've seen only Antonio gets my vote as a gentleman."

"Is that the Mexican in the saloon?" Bernice crammed another peppermint into her mouth. Although she pretended to be tough, she was still young.

"Yes, that's him. I want you to come with us, but I won't force you." Sabrina scowled at Cade. "Nor will Mr. Brody. We only want to help."

"Yeah, well I can take better care of myself than he can. The man don't even know how to boil turnips." Bernice snorted, drawing a chuckle from Sabrina.

Cade couldn't exactly be insulted. After all, the girl was right. He'd moved out to the wilderness without knowing how to make anything but trouble.

"Let's just get to town before the snow really starts blowing. I don't know about you two but I don't fancy being up on a horse in a blizzard." He turned away, feeling just as mixed up as he was before they found the girl.

Quiet female murmurs followed behind him as he walked to the cabin. The snow was getting heavier by the minute, thick flakes that sat in piles on his shoulders. The storm grew in intensity while the wind's howling began to resemble a pack of wolves.

By the time he got to the cabin, his fingers were completely numb. Same went for his toes. He'd spent time in snowy climates before but this was ridiculous. This was *mountain* snow, and it was as fierce as he was.

The cabin was marginally warmer, but he hadn't put more wood on the fire so what was left was not much more than ashes. He cursed heartily then reached into the wood bin for some kindling. The girls were just coming into the cabin, looking like the ghosts Jeremiah claimed to see. The snow had turned them both lily white.

"I've got to get the damn wood for the fire." He walked outside without waiting for a response. Time was short and he needed to get both of them out of his house and out of his life, as fast as possible.

Sabrina stared at the closed door and wondered how she'd gotten so involved with the man. He was obstinate, sarcastic and childish, not to mention intolerant and frustrating. Yet, damn it all, she still liked him, a lot, perhaps even a whole lot more than she should, bordering on the other "L" word.

Maybe it was due to the fact that although he showed the world a cold, calculating man, he also had done a lot she considered kind and considerate. He blustered and complained, yet he'd still saved Jeremiah's life and had come into Eustace to ask Sabrina's help to save Bernice.

Those were not the actions of a man who didn't care about anyone or anything, no matter how much he protested. Even as her stomach tumbled along with her heart with confusion, she led Bernice over to the fire and stirred the embers and the kindling.

"It's not very warm in here." The girl gestured with her arm. "He dirtied it up pretty good though."

"What do you mean?" Sabrina looked around and just noticed the clothes lying on the chair, the ashes on the floor and the dirty pot on the stove.

"Old Louie kept this place neat as a pin. After he passed, I kept it nice." She turned a hard gaze on Sabrina. "Until that gunslinger came here and ruined everything."

Sabrina'd had no idea the child had been living in the cabin. No wonder Cade felt as if he owed the child something, or perhaps he hadn't known he'd kicked her out of her home. Then the word gunslinger echoed in her head again. She'd had a feeling Cade was hiding something dark, and Bernice had seen what Sabrina couldn't.

"What makes you think he's a gunslinger?" she asked

as casually as she could, her heart pounding in anticipation of the answer.

"He looked like a greenhorn to me, wearing britches that were too short, and so I helped him a bit with water and vegetables. He's an ungrateful bastard." The girl curled her upper lip in an expression so much like Cade's, Sabrina was hard-pressed to smother the chuckle that threatened.

"But what about the gunslinger part?"

"Oh, that. Well, you see, the first day he got here, he walked out to the woods and buried something. After he left, I dug it up to see what it was." She shrugged as if spying on folks was commonplace. "It was a sack with some fancy black clothes and a pair of pistols with worn grips. And I seen him move like a gunslinger, reaching for a gun that ain't on his hip no more. Mark my words, that man is a gunslinger."

She crossed her arms over her chest and nodded, a sage in the guise of a thirteen-year-old girl.

However, everything she said made sense. All the questions Sabrina had about his behavior, attitude and actions were answered by Bernice's observations. Many men came west to make a new life for themselves, and Cade was apparently one of them. She had no doubt that Cade Brody was a made-up name, something pulled from nowhere and pinned to his chest to pretend he wasn't who he really was.

Was she angry? No, but hurt and confused for certain. Sabrina had feelings for the man, and she didn't even know who he really was. An inner voice argued that she knew exactly who he was inside, which was all that mattered.

"Where in tarnation is he? It's colder than a well-digger's ass in here." Bernice apparently knew much more than how to survive in the wilderness alone. Being a miner's child, she'd picked up many colorful expressions.

It had been more than ten minutes since Cade had gone out for wood. The girl was right, where was he? Sabrina headed for the door, hoping he'd be on the other side of it, but he wasn't. She glanced back at Bernice.

"Please stay here. Can you do that for me?"

Bernice rolled her eyes. "I reckon, but I ain't made up my mind yet about going to town with ya."

"That's fine, but for now I need to know you'll stay here where it's safe. I don't want to worry about both of you."

The expression on the girl's face made Sabrina realize no one had ever worried about her before. Sabrina's heart pinched at the thought, and she vowed Bernice would never feel that way again.

"I'll be back in a minute or two." Sabrina stepped outside and the snow pelted her face. She pulled her scarf tight around her head and chin, covering her nose and mouth until she could breathe without a mouthful of snow. When she turned toward the woodpile at the back of the cabin, she saw nothing but white. Cade was gone.

Chapter Eight

Sabrina's mouth went dry beneath the wool scarf. Where was he? The snowstorm was picking up speed and intensity by the second. He'd already admitted he was not experienced in the outdoors, so where in the world would he have gone?

She called his name as loud as she could, but the wind threw it back at her. There was no way he'd hear her unless he was standing right beside her, and even then it was doubtful. She attempted to look around, trying to figure out where he was, when a brief reprieve in the wind revealed the lean-to behind the corral. Of course, he likely went to check on the horses.

With a last glance at the cabin to find Bernice looking through the window at her, Sabrina nodded and headed toward the lean-to, holding onto the corral railing as she went. It was a good thing he'd built it or a body could get lost in a storm. It seemed as if it took an hour to reach the lean-to, but it was probably two minutes. She stepped under the eave, grateful to be out of the wind. Cade's horse was munching hay and staring at her with his great brown eyes. Her palomino huddled behind the big bay, doubtless enjoying being close to a large, warm body.

Sabrina rubbed their noses. "Hey, you two, where is that man, hmm? Have you seen him? Because when I find him, I'm going to paddle his behind for making me worry about him."

A pained chuckle came from the corner. "You're worried about me?" Cade's question ended on a gasp.

She ran back out into the snow and around the horses until she got to the dark corner where she'd heard his voice. He lay in a crumpled heap, blood streaming from a gash on his forehead.

"Sweet heavens, what happened?" She tore off a piece of her petticoat and pressed it against the wound.

He hissed but didn't pull away. "My stupid horse decided I was here to take his new girlfriend away so he kicked me, hard."

"Where did he kick you?" She wanted to check him for broken bones before moving him. Clara had taught her some healing techniques, but Sabrina was definitely a novice nurse.

"In the lean-to."

She sobbed out a chuckle. "Not funny, Mr. Brody. Let me help you back into the house."

"I don't know if I can stand. I tried it a minute ago and that's when the side of the building decided to hit my head." He shifted on the ground. "But my ass is nearly frozen through so I guess I need to try again."

"Don't worry, I'm not a fragile creature, Cade. I won't

break." She swallowed the rush of caring feelings at the thought that he was truly hurt and might have died if she hadn't come looking for him. It confirmed her suspicion that what she felt for him was much more than like. "Can you hold this cloth to your wound for me? I need both arms free."

"Sure thing, darlin'. I'd like you to wrap your arms around me." His speech was slurring, a sure sign he'd hit his head quite hard.

With quite a few grunts, curses and splinters, Sabrina got him up and walking toward the house. She took a lot of his weight, grateful the snow was only a few inches deep, which made their slow progress a bit easier. More than once, he stopped and hung onto the corral for a few moments, before she urged him to walk. Again it seemed the cabin was a mile away, and each second she felt him shudder in the cold made it that much more urgent to get him inside.

Just when Sabrina thought they'd never make it, Bernice appeared and tucked herself under Cade's right arm, forcing him to let go of the corral fence.

"What are you doing, girl?" he managed to get out.

"Helping, you idiot." She was surprisingly strong and lifted some of the burden off Sabrina. "Now walk."

Although they seemed to bring out the worst in each other, Bernice and Cade had some kind of unspoken bond. Sabrina sensed it running beneath their snide chatter. Something bound them together, gave them an understanding of each other. She didn't pretend to understand it, but was thankful for it.

When they finally made it to the door, Bernice got it open and they side-stepped Cade inside. By then he'd passed out, a dead weight of at least one hundred seventy pounds. Sabrina had never been so glad she was a big-boned girl.

"Let's get him to the bed."

They practically dragged him to the bed, panting and grunting. Sabrina's muscles screamed in protest with every step, but they made it and managed not to drop him like a sack of potatoes. He laid there, vulnerable and looking pale beneath the frozen blood on his face. Sabrina's heart twisted at the sight. Oh boy, she was definitely in trouble.

"I'll go get some wood. We'll need to get him undressed so I can examine him for wounds."

Bernice's blonde eyebrows shot up. "You want to get him naked?"

Sabrina's cheeks heated. "You never mind about his clothes for now, just get his boots and hat off. Make sure the bandage stays on his head and I'll do the rest."

"If'n you say so." Bernice glanced down at the man with doubt. "I hope his feet don't stink."

Sabrina left the cabin, almost absurdly appreciative of the cold snow as it pelted her hot face. She carried four armfuls of wood to the door and then added four more just in case. By the time she had finished that chore, she was marginally more in control of herself.

When she opened the door with an armful of wood,

Bernice met her halfway and took some of the wood from her. "'Bout time you got back. I was ready to conk him on the head again to get some peace and quiet."

"You need a firm hand and some well-deserved spanking, little girl," Cade snarled from the bed.

"I was only gone ten minutes."

"It was twenty." Bernice shut the door against the snow and wind. "I know because I counted every second."

"I was stocking up on wood in case the snow decides to stick around for a while." She dropped the wood in the box next to the fireplace. "I need to get more."

"Let me do it. You take care of the gunslinger." Bernice headed for the door before Sabrina could answer.

Cade had to have the last word. "Stop calling me that."

Sabrina shook her head and took a moment to remove her coat, scarf and boots. Just being in the same room again with him made her stomach tighten and her skin tingle. She was no green girl, but her body sure acted like one.

"I'm going to put some water on to boil." She needed to focus on helping him and not on her discomfort, or whatever it was.

"If you need bandages, there's a few rags in the bucket near the sink." Cade was at last helpful.

Familiar chores soothed Sabrina and by the time the water was hot, she was calm again. Bernice had brought in two nice stacks of wood and was currently sitting on the one chair at the table glaring at Cade. He had his eyes closed, apparently unconscious again.

Sabrina checked the rags, surprised to find them clean, then took the lot of them and a basin of hot water over to Cade. The cut on his forehead was superficial, much to her relief. Head wounds tended to bleed a lot, and she was glad for the cold since it helped stop the flow of blood. Without any medicines or even a poultice, the best she could do was keep it clean and wrap a bandage around his head.

She opened his shirt as gently as she could, wincing when she saw the clear hoofprint on his ribs.

"That bad?" His beautiful dark eyes regarded her for the first time without the mask of indifference he usually presented.

"It's ugly." She pressed the area around the wound. "Does it hurt?"

"Does a bear shit in the woods? Of course it hurts." Back to his usual crotchety self, Cade hissed like a snake.

"I think it's just bruised ribs. I can bandage them for you, which will help, but I'm afraid they're going to hurt for a while." She ran her fingers on the smooth skin.

"You know if you keep that up, I'm going to think you want to be more than my nurse." He pierced her with a glance that could boil water by itself.

Her heart stuttered even as she continued to touch him. "I'm just checking your wounds. That horse has a hard kick."

"Not nearly as hard as Bernice's mouth." He shot a

glare in the girl's direction.

Sabrina reached up and turned his chin back to her. "Don't worry about Bernice. Let's get you bandaged up so we can get you in to town and see Clara."

He made a face. "She doesn't like me."

Sabrina laughed. "Clara can be like a porcupine at times, but she's a wonderful person and a good healer." She gestured to his shirt. "Can you sit up so we can wrap your ribs?"

He took a deep breath then nodded. "Let's get this over with."

Each grunt of pain, each tightening of his muscles, shot through Sabrina's body too. She knew every movement she made to help him actually hurt him. It wasn't as if she were trying to cause him harm—on the contrary—but she couldn't help feeling guilty. When she finally tied off the bandage, he sucked in another pained breath and sat back.

"Jesus, I need a drink." His voice was hoarse, full of numerous kinds of pain. He laughed without humor, then gasped. "Shit, that hurts."

"I'm sorry, Cade. You don't have any laudanum here, do you?" She knew it was a slim hope, but she felt like they had to do something.

Bernice appeared next to the bed. "I can rustle up some willow bark for tea."

Sabrina wiped her face, surprised to find tears on her cheeks. "I didn't know you were a healer."

Bernice shrugged. "Just something I learned from a woman that once lived with my pa. It helped when I hurt my hand one time in the chute."

That statement told Sabrina the girl had helped her father with the mine, regardless of what he'd told everyone. Not only that, but she'd been hurt. One day Sabrina would have to talk to the young woman about it, but not now. Cade's health was more important.

"I don't know about you going back out in this snow." Sabrina glanced at the window, at the snow blowing past horizontally.

"It grows right at the edge of the forest. I can get some and be back in ten minutes. Better than either one of you did outside." Bernice might have sounded boastful any other time, but Sabrina believed every word she said. The child had survived on her own for almost a year.

"I can't stop you, but I can ask you to be careful. Take the lantern with you if you'd like."

"She can just shoot fire from her mouth if she needs light." Cade smirked at the girl.

"Very funny, gunslinger." She grabbed her too-large coat and headed for the door.

"Stop calling me that."

"Gunslinger."

Sabrina rolled her eyes at them since they were acting like a pair of five-year-olds with their taunting and name-calling. "Bernice, the sooner you go, the better. I don't think the storm is going to wait for you."

"Fine, I'm going." A swirl of snow came in as she went out.

Sabrina glanced at Cade, his complexion pasty in the orange light from the fire. "I'm sorry you got hurt."

"Stupid horse. Ornery cuss tried to bite me a few days ago." Cade closed his eyes.

"Maybe he'd be better if you gave him a name." She stood, needing to put some space between them. As she busied herself getting fresh water to clean the bloody rags from his head wound, she thought he'd fallen asleep.

She was wrong.

"Horse doesn't need a name."

"Yes he does. You need to form a bond with him and that won't happen unless he knows he's your horse. Give him a name." Sabrina didn't know why it was important she convince him, but it was.

"I don't want to bond with him." Cade was nothing if not stubborn.

"You need to bond with someone. If it's not going to be me, it might as well be that horse. He'll be your only company soon since you came here to be alone." She heard the pain in her voice and cursed her soft heart.

Cade was silent for a few minutes before he spoke again. "She's right, you know. I'm a gunslinger. You'd do best to forget about me, Sabrina. You deserve a man without a past like mine."

Sabrina could have shouted with joy to finally hear truth coming from his mouth. "You have no right to tell me what I deserve or what I should do."

"No, I don't but that ain't gonna stop me. I'm not a good man. I've killed people for money and spent it on whores and whiskey." He sounded so full of self-hatred, tears pricked her eyes.

"I don't care what you did before you came here."

"You should."

Sabrina squeezed the water out of the rag and spread it out on the edge of the wooden sink. When she felt in control of her emotions, she walked back to Cade, and knew what she wanted, *needed* to do.

He opened his eyes, their depths full of unnamed darkness. "Leave while you can."

She ignored his hoarse whisper. "No." Kneeling down, she settled next to him and cupped his face in her hands. "I'm afraid it's not that easy to get rid of me."

"Sabrina." Her name was torn from his throat, and she could see the struggle within him. He wanted her to leave, but he had no choice. Sabrina controlled the situation and she chose not to.

For better or for worse, Sabrina was there to stay.

"I'm not the saint you think I am." She took a deep breath, ready to tell Cade her deepest shame. "I've done things I'm not proud of."

"Like what, give someone the wrong change?"

She frowned at his biting words. "You know, when Eric and I married, it was convenient. He wanted a wife, I wanted a husband. Ellen was already engaged to Whit

Dawson, who worked at the mill with Eric."

"Your husband didn't tend the store?" He sounded surprised.

"No, Eric worked with his hands. He loved being outdoors." She closed her eyes and pictured his freckled face and easy smile. "He was a good man who couldn't help who he fell in love with."

"You're an easy woman to love."

Sabrina's heart skipped a beat. "He didn't love me, he loved Ellen."

She let that sink in before she continued. "I didn't know until after he was dying. God, I was so blind." Pain washed through her. "Whit found out, you see, when he saw them talking together one night at the mill. He went crazy and fought with Eric while Ellen watched."

Cade's hand touched hers. "What happened, Brina?"

Sabrina took in a shaky breath. "Whit stabbed him in the chest while she watched, then cut up her face so no man would ever want her again. There was s-so much blood."

He squeezed her hand. "Were you there?"

"No, but Jeremiah came and got me. I arrived just before Eric died, with a bleeding Ellen sobbing over his body." She closed her eyes at the memory. "I never knew. I was so stupid that I never guessed they loved each other."

"Did they fall in love before or after you were married?"

"Does it matter?" Sabrina could only wonder. "It cost

them both so much. Eric lost his life and Ellen might as well have lost hers for all the living she's done in the last five years."

"Jesus, you think that's your fault? Hell, your husband was cheating on you—"

"They never cheated."

"With his heart he was, don't you dare tell me different." Cade's fierce expression told her he cared she'd been hurt, which was surprising and amazing. "You were the victim here, not them. They chose to be together, chaste or not, and got caught."

Sabrina tried not to think about what Eric and Ellen had done or hadn't done. In thought or deed, they had forsaken her.

"They suffered more than I ever did," she said quietly.

"What happened to Whit?"

"He ran, never came back. Without a regular lawman there was nothing we could do." She looked into Cade's dark eyes. "I was angry, so angry at God, at Eric, at Ellen, at everyone. I didn't speak to her for a year."

Those dark days following Eric's death were the lowest point in Sabrina's life. In the end, she found the will to come back from the hellish pit she had existed in and started to live again.

"You forgave."

Sabrina nodded. "I did because I had to. Forgiving them was the only way to release myself from the constant anger and hurt."

Cade lowered his gaze to their joined hands. "I wish I had your strength. I can never forgive anyone, not even myself."

✧

Cade wanted to get his ass out of the cabin and ride hell for leather into Eustace with the two females currently driving him loco. The snow had been flying for twelve hours and full dark had turned the trip foolhardy and dangerous, yet he still wanted to leave.

An army of ants were crawling up and down his skin as he lay there with his ribs screaming and head pounding. Not only that, but he had to suffer through Sabrina taking care of him as if he were a precious possession. Then there was Bernice, the eighty-year-old woman in the body of a teenage girl.

He couldn't imagine a deeper hell than being trapped with them until spring.

Sabrina fluttered around, cooking up soup with turnips, of course, and biscuits that smelled like sunshine. Bernice glared at him from the kitchen while she peppered Sabrina with questions. Somebody who didn't know him might think they were one big happy family.

Cade hurt himself when he snorted.

"Are you all right?" Sabrina paused in the middle of cutting out the biscuits with a tin cup. A spot a flour glowed white on her left cheek.

His heart stuttered at the sight of the concern in her eyes. Dammit to hell, why did it have to be snowing? Why couldn't she just have left when he told her to?

"I'd be much better if the two of you would stop yammering and leave me the hell alone." He sounded like a goddamn bully, for pity's sake.

"Nice try, but it won't work." Sabrina went back to the biscuits.

Bernice continued to eyeball him. "He needs a muzzle."

Unbelievably, Cade stuck out his tongue at the pint-sized curmudgeon. She sniffed and turned away, leaving him to his self-imposed misery. A tiny voice deep inside nudged him, whispering he wanted the happy family in front of him.

Jesus, he really was going loco.

"So where are you from, gunslinger?"

"I'm not talking to you if you can't stop nagging me."

"I ain't nagging. I'm just curious. You musta growed up in a city 'cause you don't know shit about living out here." Bernice smirked, daring Cade to contradict her.

"Just because I'm not a mountain man doesn't mean I can't do anything, and you need to watch your language, little girl." Her evaluation of him was, once again, dead on.

"Ha, I knew I was right." Smug too.

"Fine, I lived in cities all my life until this year. I can swing a hammer, rope a cattle and even clean hooves. I ain't much of a cook, but I can ride like the wind and I'm fast with...other things too." Cade didn't know why he felt the need to justify himself to the girl, but he did anyway.

"Fast with other things? Like guns?" Bernice looked so damn sure of herself, Cade's temper flew out of control.

He launched himself off the bed, pleased to see a flash of fear in her eyes. Pain roared through his chest and he could hardly catch a breath, but he was determined.

"Cade, what are you doing?" Sabrina rushed over to him, her flour-covered hands leaving smears on his skin.

"I'm going to paddle her ass." He headed for Bernice, who screeched and ran for the door.

"Don't you dare leave this cabin, young lady." Sabrina sounded so fierce, even Cade stopped in his tracks. Wielding authority was yet another side to the complex woman, along with the shaking widow he'd comforted in the firelight. He wasn't sure if he liked the bossy one or not.

"He's gonna hit me." The girl had her hand on the latch, ready to run into the howling snowstorm rather than face his wrath.

Since when did he go around threatening thirteen year olds? What the hell was wrong with him?

"I'm not going to hurt you." He met Sabrina's gaze and saw something he hadn't expected, understanding.

"Why don't you put a shirt on and I'll make you some coffee to go with the biscuits?" She was nothing if not cheerful.

Dammit.

"Fine. I'll sit at the table too. I'm tired of lying on that stupid bed like an invalid." As he snatched the clean shirt off the hook on the wall, Sabrina's warm hands landed on his back. A shudder of pure longing wracked him. God how he wanted her, and not just in his bed. It was much more than that.

"Let me help you."

He didn't protest, he simply allowed her to slip on the shirt, relishing her touch and concern. Only one person had ever made his way past his hard shell to his heart. Brett Malloy had become a friend for life. However, no woman had even come close. Cade was scared, terrified for God's sake. His urge to leave the cabin grew to enormous proportions until he could hardly stand there one more second.

She met his gaze and he wondered what she saw in the dark depths of his eyes. A sad smile graced her beautiful mouth.

"I won't hurt you, I promise," she whispered a second before she kissed him.

Cade closed his eyes, certain he'd do something stupid like cry if he kept them open. "No, but I'll hurt you."

A small sigh gusted past his cheek. He couldn't look at her, just couldn't.

"Have it your way, Mr. Brody." She buttoned his shirt with crisp movements. "Just so you realize I'm not giving up that easily."

That's exactly what he was afraid of. Or was the fear a disguise for hope?

The snow let up in the morning, leaving a blanket of white that sparkled like diamonds in the sun. The bright blue in the sky seemed impossible after the horrendous storm, almost mocking the weather. Sabrina didn't care if the storm was over or not, she knew it was the signal for Cade to get back to Eustace.

She didn't want to go. Being in the cabin, taking care of him, even making biscuits ignited a longing so deep, she could taste the tang on her tongue. She'd been married, had a home and a husband, but this was different. Beneath the everyday tasks like washing dishes and setting the table lurked a contentment she'd never known, as if this were what she was meant to do.

Somehow in the last month, she'd fallen in love with Cade Brody, an admitted gunslinger with a grumpy disposition and a burning need to be left alone. The connection between them had been immediate and intense. She knew he felt it too, which was why he pushed her away.

She'd cared for her husband, a sweet emotion that resembled a friendship more than a passion. What she felt for Cade was deeper, rougher, more elemental. It involved not only her heart, but her head and soul as well. She felt consumed by the need to learn more about him and be with him.

When he'd confessed to being an ex-gunslinger, which

obviously haunted him, she'd felt closer to him. Cade had tried to push her away, but instead he had pulled her closer. It seemed backwards, but to Sabrina, it made perfect sense. He felt comfortable enough to reveal such a dark thing about himself.

Sabrina had suffered pain, loneliness and betrayal in her life. The night before she'd felt safe enough with Cade to share those memories with him. Judging by his behavior though, he wasn't ever going to forgive himself or give their relationship a chance. If only he wasn't so stubborn. Well, then he wouldn't be himself and that was who she fell in love with.

The coffee bubbled in the pot on the stove, reminding her that daydreams solved nothing. She turned away from the window and found Cade watching her. He'd pulled the shirt on, but he'd only done up three buttons on the bottom and they were misaligned. His dark hair stuck up like a witch's broom. Darned if her heart didn't stutter at the sight of him in the morning, just rising from his bed.

"Good morning." She picked up a cup and focused on the coffee instead of the sexy man who didn't want to be with her.

"That ain't necessarily true." He stepped up beside her. "What makes you think it's good?"

She ignored the expanse of chest revealed by the half-buttoned shirt. The very sight of it made her fingers itch to touch him, perhaps even nibble. Then she smelled his soap, a fresh clean scent that for some reason enticed her more.

"For one thing, it's stopped snowing and for another, there doesn't appear to be any damage from the storm."

"At least not yet. My ribs and back are gonna kill me after I shovel a path to the damn horses." He thrust an empty cup at her.

"You can't shovel snow with injured ribs." She couldn't even fathom why he'd think it was possible.

"They're just bruised." He pushed at her shoulder until she faced him. His dark brows were in an angry V on his forehead. "I am taking you two back to Eustace if I have to kill myself doing it."

Sabrina swallowed his proclamation with all the bitterness he put into it. It hurt more than she expected. Every woman hopes the man she falls in love with will return the favor. However it seemed she picked the one man who would only regard her as a nuisance and do his best to be rid of her as quickly as possible.

"You're a bastard." She slapped the coffee cup out of his hand, and it tinged on the floor with a hollow sound.

"You got that right. My ma fucked so many men she didn't know who'd left her with a squalling brat." The ancient pain in his voice was only matched by the rancor that accompanied it.

Sabrina didn't know whether to be shocked or saddened by his confession about his mother's sexual habits. She couldn't imagine growing up knowing her mother had been promiscuous, or that apparently it was common knowledge.

"I'm sure she didn't think you were a squalling—"

He stuck his finger in her face. "Don't. *Don't* even fucking think about judging me."

"I wasn't going to. If you'd stop cussing at me and listen—"

Cade picked up the coffeepot with his bare hand and threw it against the fireplace. Hot brew splattered everywhere like a dark bloodstain while the fire hissed and spat smoke. Sabrina stared at the mess, wondering how the situation had gotten so far out of control in moments.

Bernice appeared in the doorway with an armful of wood. "I guess coffee ain't gonna happen." She kicked the door closed with her foot and stepped around them.

Sabrina's breath was trapped somewhere in her throat with her heart. Cade had never looked so frightening or so frightened. She reached for him and he pulled away, his face twisted in a mask of self-loathing and fury.

"I'm never going to hate you." Her words trembled almost as much as the rest of her. She'd felt a great many bad things before, but none of them were as painful as what she felt in the face of Cade's agony.

"Then I pity you." His expression hardened into stone. "We're leaving in ten minutes." With that, he snatched his coat from the hook on the wall and slammed out the door.

Sabrina's heart thumped in her ears as loud as a bass drum, as if she'd run from one end of New Mexico and back. Every muscle in her body was tight, almost to the point of pain. If anyone touched her at that moment, she might shatter into a thousand pieces.

She didn't know how long it took her to get her breath back, but Bernice had time to load up the wood box until it was full.

"You about done? I think that man is fixing to leave without us." The girl sounded matter-of-fact, not pitying or accusing, which helped ease the sting of her words.

"I think so. I just... I've never... Oh I don't know what I'm saying." Sabrina's shock and hurt gave way to anger, a deeper, stronger emotion that sustained her through the walk out to the lean-to. Although she knew he was there, waiting to hurl hurtful words, she marched on, determined.

The slap of cold air made her eyes sting, along with the sun on the white snow. The pain reminded her that life went on even as she'd gasped for air minutes ago. Cade had meant to push her away, to cause irreparable damage to whatever relationship they'd built. He almost succeeded.

The horses were saddled and Cade was just tightening the cinch on his horse. The bay reached around and tried to bite him, earning a chuckle from Bernice.

"Stupid fucking horse." Cade pushed at the equine's great head. "Stop trying to eat me."

Sabrina took Felicidad's reins and led the horse away from him. "I think it's a natural reaction," she tossed over her shoulder.

"What about my things?" Bernice petted the mare's nose. "I got a mule and stuff I don't want to leave to the scavengers."

A dramatic sigh sounded from the other side of the gelding. "Where's the mule?"

"Over yonder." Bernice pointed to the dense forest. "About a fifteen minute walk."

"Jesus please us." Cade threw himself up into the saddle with a grunt, his black hat hiding his expression from them. Sabrina knew he must be in pain. His ribs barely had twelve hours to heal from the horse kick. "Then we best go get your brother."

"That mule ain't my brother." Bernice scowled at him.

He snorted. "Oh, you mean it's not stubborn, mean and impossible?"

"Well, a'course he is. All mules are."

"Exactly." Cade turned the horse toward the trees. "Let's get moving then."

Sabrina helped the girl up on the saddle, then mounted behind her. Felicidad shifted under the weight of both of them.

"Shhh. It's okay, girl, she's a friend." Sabrina patted the mare's neck until she settled down. Cade had almost reached the tree line before they started off behind him.

"He's an ornery cuss, ain't he?" Bernice humphed. "If I was his woman, I'd make him pay for what he done."

Sabrina swallowed the spurt of pain at the girl's words. She had no idea how much Cade had actually hurt Sabrina, or how much she wanted to make him pay for it. However it would be spiteful and vengeful to follow through on the thought. Sabrina wanted to maintain her dignity and would only do so by ignoring his childish, hurtful words.

Their breath came out in white puffs in the crisp morning air. Once they caught up with Cade, he gestured with his arm for them to precede him.

"I don't know where the hell I'm going." He turned his face away when Sabrina caught his eye.

Coward.

"It's north." Bernice pointed to the densest part of the trees. "Over the ridgeline and around the side of the hill."

"I wouldn't expect any less." Cade was determined to be as obnoxious as possible that day.

"Never mind the fool behind us," Sabrina told Bernice. "Let's just get your things so we can get to town."

Her heart still ached from the blows rendered by Cade's words, but Sabrina held on, never letting him see just how badly she hurt. The ride to Bernice's home was a blur of blinking back tears and swallowing them into the darkest regions of her soul. The farther they traveled, the colder it got, yet Sabrina ignored it. She would be strong.

"There's the hill. It's just around the other side." Bernice pointed again and Sabrina urged the mare around the base of the small hill.

When they reached the other side, a rickety shack was barely visible beneath the thick pines surrounding it. A firepit sat outside with a pot hanging from the spit above it. It was neat, yet obviously the girl had next to nothing. She climbed down from the horse and headed for the shack.

"I need to get Lucky and pack my stuff on her."

"Do you want some help?" Sabrina called as Bernice disappeared into the shack.

"No. Don't got much, so it won't take but a minute or two."

Sabrina was painfully aware of Cade sitting on his horse behind her, staring holes into her back by the feel of it. The bone-numbing cold had reached up her riding skirt and grabbed hold of every inch of her body. Her teeth started chattering, and she longed for the warmth of the sun they'd left in the meadow.

"You're cold."

"You're astute."

"I don't know what that word means, but I think you insulted me." His horse neighed and she heard him murmuring to the beast. No doubt he'd scented the mule, wherever it was.

"I don't think it's possible to insult you, Mr. Brody." Her words were as crisp as the air around them.

"I think you'd be surprised what insults me." He nudged the horse up beside her, practically daring her to look at him.

"I don't care to know." Her hands and feet were numb, as was her nose and chin. The frigid air started to seep into her bones.

"Here, take the damn thing." Cade thrust something at her, dangling it under her nose. "I can't stand to hear your teeth clack together anymore."

Sabrina looked down to find a handmade scarf in his hands. It was a thick, crocheted piece in a startling midnight blue, almost black. She couldn't help but reach out and take it.

"It's beautiful." She fingered the tight stitches. "Someone must have really loved you to make it."

His laugh made the hairs on the back of her neck stand up. "Not hardly. That was a gift from a friend's mother. She'd made it for one of her boys but gave it to me instead. The love was meant for someone else."

There it was again, that echo of ancient pain dredged up from within him. She took off her hat and wrapped the scarf around her head and ears, then her neck, the warmth of the wool not nearly as comforting as his scent trapped within the fibers. As she put the hat back on her head, settling it around the scarf, she breathed in deeply, somehow drawing strength from the wool.

"Thank you."

He grunted and stepped his horse back away from her. "It wasn't a kindness. I was tired of hearing your teeth clatter."

"Liar." Sabrina finally turned and looked at him, catching him staring at her. The longing, the absolute naked longing in his eyes made her heart pound. He quickly shuttered his gaze, but it was too late. She'd seen what lurked behind those black eyes and it gave her the one thing she needed most.

Hope.

Chapter Nine

Cade had spent some miserable days in his life, most of which he cared not to even remember. This Sunday would be etched in his memory for the rest of his life. He'd seen something in Sabrina's eyes that scared the hell out of him, made him bare his teeth and bite her until she bled. God, he'd never wanted to hurt her, not in a million years, yet he'd deliberately slashed at her with his tongue until she was down, then he'd kicked her.

He knew he wasn't a good person, never even pretended to be one, yet she saw something in him that made her believe he was good. Cade had no clue what it could possibly be, yet she did. Bernice had no illusions as to his character and treated him appropriately. As she walked out of the hovel leading the ugliest mule he'd ever seen, she glared at him.

"Lucky might not be pretty but she's got a good soul, which is more than I can say for you, gunslinger," she snapped.

If Bernice called him gunslinger in town, he'd have to gag her. "I didn't say a word, girl. Now get up on that beast and let's get out of these trees. It's too damn cold to be jawing out here."

"I was fixing to do that anyway." She climbed up on the mule's back and the damn thing didn't protest a whit. In his experience, the ornery creatures were nothing but trouble and nobody in their right mind would ride one. Then again, he was talking about Bernice, which explained it.

Cade avoided looking at Sabrina, knowing she wore the scarf Mrs. Malloy had given him right before he left Wyoming. He'd tried to give it to Brett, but he wouldn't accept it. Told him his mama had given Cade a gift and he'd best accept it. Cade had no experience with friends or family, so when the Malloys overwhelmed him, as they often did, he'd go and hide for a few hours until they left. Brett seemed to understand that, giving him a place to work and live for the best four months of his life.

Yet Cade's past had reared its ugly head, putting Brett and his family at risk. Cade knew he'd had to leave, yet up until then, it had been the hardest thing he'd ever done. Living on the Square One Ranch had felt like home, a place he'd never found before. God knows he didn't deserve that kind of peace, and it was as short-lived as he'd expected it to be.

Now he was stuck again, this time with a woman who'd snatched his heart from his chest, a heart he hadn't known existed until six months earlier. The Malloys had discovered his heart, and Sabrina made it beat.

Cade itched to get rid of it, to go back to living life as a hollow man with nothing but his sorry self for company. It seemed as though God had other ideas for him since he'd thrown a woman to love in his path and a girl to drive him insane. Neither one of them knew what sort of havoc they wreaked within him, and if he had his way, they never would.

As they emerged from the forest into the meadow, he could breathe again, free from the confines of the damn trees. They rode ahead of him, talking quietly in the still morning, the cloudy white puffs from their breath hanging in the air. He wanted to be right there, between them, around them. God, he could almost taste the raw need to be loved by someone, anyone.

He shouldn't have pushed Sabrina away, but it had been self-defense, pure and simple. It was as if his brain and his heart had stopped speaking to each other. While his heart screamed for her, his brain pushed her away so hard it made him stop breathing. He was a complete wreck, both physically and emotionally. His head ached from the lean-to, his ribs hurt like hell from the stupid horse kick and his heart was in a vat of pain so deep he didn't think it would ever emerge.

Cade opened his mouth to talk at least a dozen times on the ride to Eustace, but he didn't, or couldn't. He didn't know which. When they arrived, he knew it was his last chance to apologize to Sabrina for what he'd said and done or risk losing her forever. He wanted to kick his own ass for the way he'd behaved the last twenty-four hours. Jesus, what a complete bastard he'd been.

As the buildings came into view, he knew it was now

or never. Seemingly of their own accord, his knees nudged the bay into a trot until he caught up with Sabrina. She stared straight ahead, refusing it seemed to look at him.

"Mr. Brody." Her tone was clipped, harsh and he deserved every second of it.

"Sabrina." Gravelly and uncertain, his voice broke. She whipped her head around and peered at him from beneath the brim of her hat. Her beautiful blue eyes gave him the strength to go on. "I wanted to say I'm so—"

"How dare you?" Sam Fuller shouted from the street in front of them, spoiling the moment and his apology.

"Sam, what's going on?" Sabrina demanded.

Sam pointed his thick finger at Cade. "That man is a liar. His name isn't even Cade Brody. He took you against your will to his cabin and apparently made you part of his brood." His nasty gaze settled on Bernice, sitting regally atop her ugly mule. "Let me guess, this is his child bride."

Bernice snorted. "I remember you. You're that loudmouthed fool from the mill."

Cade wanted to smile at her sassiness, but found that he couldn't. Sam Fuller was about to reveal his secrets to the entire town. Folks poked their heads out of doorways and windows. The small population started to gather behind the lumberman. Ellen stood on the steps of the store, piercing Cade with a fierce glare. Sabrina's sister would never accept him, but at this point, finding out why she didn't like him wasn't a task he wanted to take on.

"You'd best watch your language, young lady." Sam glanced at the crowd behind him. "Cade Brody's real name is Kincaid and he's a gunslinger with a reputation a mile long. He's killed more than a hundred men, most as a gun for hire." The malice in the other man's face was almost as bad as the shock on Sabrina's.

Frenchie, that foolish, stinky miner, stood on the steps by Ellen, a grin and a snicker emanating from his gap-toothed mouth. "I knew'd it."

Sabrina climbed down from Felicidad and walked toward Sam, trampling what was left of Cade's stupid heart beneath her boots.

When she slapped Sam, the silence descended on everyone. Cade's mouth even dropped open.

"You are a fool, Sam Fuller. Bernice was right about you." She pointed to the girl. "This is Bernice Wilkinson. Do you remember her? Her pa died of consumption at Clara's last year." She glanced at Cade, and he was relieved beyond measure to see righteous fury in her eyes. "Mr. Brody found the girl and wanted to help her into town before winter hit and he asked for my help, which I gladly gave. We found her yesterday just before the storm."

Sam's expression hardened as she spoke, her words growing louder and firmer.

"He might have a past but who doesn't? Cade is a good man, no matter what you think, Sam. I'd rather spend one night in his arms then a lifetime listening to you preach about the sins of others, while you hide your own under the rug."

When Sam slapped her, Cade didn't remember getting

off the horse, yet he was running toward them, even as Sam took Sabrina's arm in his grasp. A well-dressed man in a black suit stood by the steps to the store, a gun belt hanging from his hips.

"Let go of me." She tried to pull away, but Sam tightened his hand. "You're hurting me."

"You whore. How dare you lay with this man?" Sam raised his hand to slap her again when Cade reached them.

He'd snatched a pistol from the stranger and although the grip was unfamiliar in Cade's hand, the weight of it wasn't. Fear blossomed in Sam's eyes as soon as the barrel pressed into his chin.

"You have about one second to get your fucking hands off her before the town sees your teeth and brains in the dirt." Cade's voice was as sharp and deadly as a knife.

Sam loosened his grip and Sabrina stepped beside Cade, her hands on his shoulder.

"Don't do it. He's behaving like an ass." She tugged at him. "Please, Cade."

"He hurt you." The sound of that slap kept echoing through Cade's head, making blood-red anger pulse through him. He'd never felt so protective of anyone before or felt the absolute need to kill someone for it.

"I'm fine, my cheek stings, but I'm more upset than anything. I don't want to see anything happen to you because of Sam's stupidity." She cupped Cade's cheek. "Please, for me, let him go."

Cade had done some hard tasks in his life, yet stepping away from Sam and releasing the hammer on the pistol had to be the most difficult one. He took a deep breath as his body shook with a thirst for vengeance. Not only had the man hurt her physically, but he'd humiliated all three of them in front of the entire town.

However, he couldn't let the man get off scot-free. Cade's fist connected with Sam's chin with a satisfying crunch. As he fell toward the ground, grim satisfaction rippled through Cade.

The stranger in black stepped up with his left palm outstretched. "I'll take that back if you don't mind." A hint of a smile was on his face.

"Sorry about that. I, just, well I needed to." As Cade handed the gun over, he glanced at Sabrina and almost melted at the love in her gaze.

"I understand completely." The man stuck out his right hand. "Marshal Johnathan Black."

Cade's heart sank at the realization the stranger was a lawman, and Sam had already given the man enough information to take him into custody if he so desired.

"You know I heard the gunslinger Kincaid died in Wyoming months ago." His dark brows rose. "So I'm guessing you can't be him and Sam's blowing hot air."

Cade was able to take a breath, grateful for the reprieve, whatever the reason. "I don't know what Sam was talking about. I'm Cade Brody and this is Sabrina Edmonds." He looked at Sabrina. "The woman who's going to marry me."

Surprise and confusion flew across her face, followed by the most beautiful smile he'd ever seen.

"Sabrina, you're getting hitched?" Marshal Black asked, obviously familiar with Eustace and its residents. "I thought Sam had you in his sights."

She tucked her arm in Cade's. "I think Sam thought so too, but you were both wrong. I was waiting for the right man."

Cade couldn't believe what he'd said or done and hell, in front of the entire goddamn town. He'd not only threatened one of their prominent citizens, he'd announced that Sabrina was going to marry him. His vision started to blur and he lost sight of the ground for a moment. She held on tight, keeping him upright until he was able to take a deep breath.

"Well it's about time." Bernice popped up beside them. "I was tired of seeing y'all fight all the time."

A laugh burst from Cade's throat, one of relief, happiness and he couldn't believe, hope. He hadn't laughed in so long, if ever, he'd forgotten what it felt like.

People dispersed as the marshal, Cade, Sabrina and Bernice walked toward Antonio's saloon. It was Cade's suggestion to ask Antonio and his mother if they'd take Bernice in. The no-nonsense woman could do wonders for the girl's sassy mouth.

Cade found out Marshal Black stopped into town three or four times a year since there was no local law in Eustace. He'd known Sabrina's husband, had even gone fishing with the man on occasion.

Cade felt sick at the thought. He was an imposter trying to fill the shoes of a dead man who apparently had no enemies and no flaws. His impromptu engagement announcement to Sabrina seemed dumber by the minute.

"Where are we going?" Bernice led her mule with the rope firmly wrapped around her small hand.

"To the saloon."

"Are you gonna drink whiskey? I thought you didn't drink no more."

"What are you, a witch? Jesus, girl, how the hell do you know these things?" Cade couldn't help but wonder how the girl knew so much about him.

"You talk to yourself and God a lot." She shrugged. "I listened."

Cade closed his eyes and pinched the bridge of his nose. The girl would drive him loco any second. Sabrina's touch brought his frustration under control.

"She was lonely, probably needed to hear someone's voice. She doesn't mean to annoy you." She took his hand in hers, their gloves gripping each other tightly.

"Says you. Bernice takes great pleasure in annoying me." He scowled at the pint-size curmudgeon.

"I think she's imitating you actually."

Cade's surprise knew no bounds. "What?"

"Oh yes, I saw it from the second she came down from the tree. I think she's been watching you for quite some time because she's got your mannerisms, your habits, even your cussing." Sabrina nodded, her blue eyes dancing with glee. "Admit it, she's just like you."

"Never gonna admit to that. I wouldn't wish that on anyone." He tried to deny Sabrina's words, but the more he thought about it, the more he realized she was right. Dead on right. Jesus, how had he missed that?

"When she was in town with her pa, Bernice was quiet and shy, never said more than a few words to anyone." Sabrina smiled. "You must have inspired her."

"She never talked? That's a dream to look forward to. You think if I don't see her anymore, she'll start to act like Antonio instead and be so nice it'll make us all sick?" Cade could only imagine.

"You did it, didn't you?" Melissa Fuller ran toward them, her frizzy hair loose and flying in the wind like a crazy flag.

"What's wrong?" Sabrina tried to stop the girl, but she side-stepped her and pushed at Cade's shoulder.

"You fell in love with her. I can see it in your eyes. You did, didn't you?" Her eyes brimmed with tears and hurt.

Cade had no idea why this girl had set her cap for him. He didn't ask for it or want it. However, he didn't want to hurt her either. "I don't know what you're talking about."

"You were mine." Melissa poked her slender finger into Cade's chest.

Pain radiated from the contact, his ribs nearly hissing from it. "Melissa, I'm twenty years older than you with a whole lot of blackness in my past. No good for a sweet girl like you." He had no idea how to stop the girl from pretending they were anything but two folks who met on the street.

"But I love you." Her tiny hands gripped his jacket. "I was going to marry you."

Cade thought she'd been grasping at straws when she mentioned it before. Jesus, he could be her father. Speaking of which, Sam Fuller stomped toward them again, retribution and a father's anger stamped on his face.

"I never gave you that idea, Melissa. We only met on the street once."

"But you like poetry too. And—and you were nice to me."

"Well he ain't nice to me and I sure as hell don't want to marry him." Bernice was not being helpful.

"What are you doing with your filthy hands on my daughter?" Sam bellowed as he pulled Melissa away.

"If you notice, she had her hands on me. I never touched the girl." Cade was glad when Sabrina stepped closer to him. Her presence, the warmth from her body, gave him strength.

"It's true, Sam. You know she's been dreaming about Cade since the second she laid eyes on him. It's a crush, nothing more." She turned a sympathetic gaze on Melissa. "She's a beautiful girl who will find a man when she's ready to be a woman."

"I don't want any man. I want Cade." Melissa started crying in earnest now, huge tears that left a path of crystals on her freckled cheeks.

Sam glared daggers at Cade. "You're destroying this town."

"Oh, he is not, Sam. Stop being such an ass. Melissa had an infatuation, which you knew about. I always made it clear I wasn't going to marry you." She shook her head. "You're destroying nothing but your reputation and your relationship with your daughter. Now go."

Sam paled at Sabrina's words. "How could you choose him over me?"

"It wasn't a choice, Sam. I do what my heart tells me to."

Bernice put her hand on Melissa's shoulder. "Believe me, he ain't worth the tears, girl."

Cade thought for a moment Sam would start in on them again, but he backed away.

"Let's go, Melissa." Sam pulled her away from Bernice's touch. "I don't want you even talking to these folks anymore."

Sabrina looked at Melissa with sadness but didn't say a word, probably knowing the emotions were too raw. Sam wasn't listening to anyone but himself. Cade just wanted the man gone, out of his sight for good. No need to examine the reasons why when it was obvious.

"But, Daddy, I love him." Melissa tried to break free of her father's grasp, but the big man was too strong for her.

"No, you can't love someone like that. He's not worth the shit on your shoes, baby girl. Now let's go." Sam hoisted his daughter over his shoulder, while she squealed in protest, crying for Cade.

The day couldn't possibly get any stranger or he might have to go be by himself like he'd told Sabrina earlier. There had been too much emotion all at once and he felt as though he'd been in a fistfight.

"Sabrina, *qué pasa?*" Antonio stepped through the saloon door, a rag in his hand. His dark gaze settled on the marshal and his jaw tightened.

"I've got a favor to ask you, *amigo.*" She glanced at Cade. "We've got to ask you."

"Why is the marshal here? I've done nothing wrong." That remark alone let Cade know his Mexican friend had had a run-in with the tall marshal once or twice.

"I'm just a bystander, Mr. Rodriguez." He tipped his hat to Sabrina. "I'll just go on and visit with Clara for a spell. I'll see you folks later."

After the man in black walked away, Antonio turned his attention back to Cade and Sabrina. "Is this the girl?" He gestured to Bernice with his thumb.

"I ain't deaf or stupid, *pendejo.*" Bernice apparently knew how to curse in Spanish too.

Antonio laughed. "I like her. Go on inside before you freeze." He took the reins of the horse and the mule from the ladies. "Cade and I will take care of the, er, animals and be inside *momentito.*"

"He's not very funny. I don't think I like him." Bernice shot a glare at the two men before she let Sabrina lead her into the saloon.

"Have you been drinking?" Cade led the bay to the corral and barn behind the building.

"What do you mean?" Antonio shut the cold out, not that it was much warmer in the barn, but at least the wind wasn't tearing their skin anymore.

"Bernice is a pain in the ass with a foul mouth and a fouler disposition." Cade had been witness to both.

"Ah, she is just blustering. A scared *niña* with no family and no home. I know this girl's father, a good customer always paid for his whiskey and his women. I think Bernice was four when he took her in." Antonio shook his head. "Her *mamá* had died at the bordello down in Maya Plata."

Cade took a minute to digest that bit of information before he spoke. His throat had tightened up at the news that Bernice was more like him than he cared to admit.

"So the miner wasn't her father?" His voice was as rough as the leather beneath his hands.

"No, but he was a good man. I don't think she knows so don't tell her."

Antonio was wrong. That girl knew exactly who her mother had been and who her father wasn't. No wonder Sabrina saw Cade's mannerisms in the girl, she earned them just as he had.

"You want her to stay with me and *Mamá, sí?*" Antonio finished rubbing down the mare and put her in a stall with oats and water. Then he started pulling off the sacks and belongings from the mule.

"She needs a home where people won't judge her for

who she is, or was, or even who her parents were." Cade closed the stall down on his bay, just missing getting bitten on the ass by the ornery horse. "Dammit. He's gonna take a chunk out of me one day."

Antonio chuckled. "You need to name your horse, you know. He can't be just 'horse' or he'll be angry at you all the time."

Cade humphed. "I don't think so. He was born a nasty horse and he'll die a nasty horse." He slapped the bay's rump, earning a disgruntled whinny. "So you'll take her in?"

Antonio scratched the little ugly mule behind the ears. "Of course we take her in. *Mamá* would love a *niña* to spoil and fuss over. Are these her things?"

Cade glanced at the sorry collection of mismatched household items including a pot, a pan, two broken wooden spoons fashioned from branches, a blanket with more holes than that fancy cheese, and some men's clothes.

"Yep, those are hers. I expect she'll want to check every item to be sure I haven't taken anything." He walked out of the barn, followed by Antonio.

"She likes you."

"Who?" Cade pretended not to know.

"Ah, you are funny, you know who I mean. The girl looks at you as if you are her papa." Antonio clipped him on the shoulder.

"Jesus, I hope not. I don't think I could be anyone's papa." Cade shuddered at the thought of any child being

187

raised by him, learning the dark secrets of life from a shattered father.

"What do you think is going to happen when you marry Sabrina? Yes, I hear the news already." Antonio opened the back door of the saloon. "Married people make babies."

The bottom of Cade's stomach hit the snow under his boots. Babies?

Sabrina settled Bernice in at a table in the back of the saloon, then went in search of fixings for tea in the kitchen. The journey into town, the cold air, not to mention the confrontations with Sam, left her with a sour taste in her mouth and a bone-weary exhaustion. She stripped off her jacket but kept the scarf wrapped around her neck. It helped remind her of the man who'd given it to her. The man who'd announced their engagement in front of the entire town. She hadn't minded though. Cade wasn't the type to ask for anything, and his behavior told her more than his words ever could. He loved her whether or not he'd admit it.

Her heart thumped hard at the memory and the possibilities of what could happen. With shaking hands, she stoked the fire in the stove, then filled the kettle with water from the pump in the sink. While she waited for the water to boil, her mind moved through the memories of the day.

It had been a topsy-turvy Sunday to say the least, and it was only two in the afternoon. In fact the whole weekend had sapped her strength.

"Sabrina, *cómo estás?*" Mrs. Rodriguez shuffled into the kitchen, a welcome smile on her wrinkled face.

Sabrina burst into tears, overwhelmed with everything. Although she was embarrassed, she couldn't seem to stop crying. The older woman took her into her arms, crooning in Spanish as she held Sabrina through a maelstrom.

The back door opened and a fresh batch of cold air brushed against her, but Sabrina didn't look up to see who it was. All she heard was Mrs. Rodriguez yelling at them to leave. Two pairs of shoes thumped past them, and Sabrina knew one of them belonged to Cade. His scent was unmistakable, and her body recognized it immediately.

"Ah, *hija, está bien, está bien.*" Mrs. Rodriguez rubbed Sabrina's back, bringing comfort where it was desperately needed.

When Sabrina felt a bit of her control returning, she accepted the lace handkerchief from the older woman and dried her face.

"*¿Pobrecita, qué pasa?*"

"I don't know what happened or at least it would be hard to explain." She shook her head. "I fell in love, thought I'd lost him, then rescued a girl and now I'm getting married."

Mrs. Rodriguez's eyebrows went up as Sabrina spoke. "*Dios mío*, Sabrina. What didn't happen to you?"

Sabrina almost laughed. "Not much."

"Who is this man, *quién es este hombre?*" The older woman looked ready to do battle with whoever had been responsible for Sabrina's tears.

"It's Cade Brody and no, he's not a bad man. I just... He's hurt deep down here." She pressed her fist against her chest. "It's an old, painful wound he's not willing to let heal. I think some awful things happened to him when he was a boy. None of that matters though because I love him."

There, she'd said it out loud and it felt good. It felt more than good, it felt *right*. Mrs. Rodriguez nodded.

"*Bueno.* He be a good husband or he answer to me." She thumped her own chest, earning a smile from Sabrina.

"*Gracias.* I don't know what I'd do without friends like you and Antonio." Sabrina meant every word of it too. Her friends were precious to her, even Sam who'd gotten it in his head to be a complete ass. It would take time to forgive him for what he'd done, however their friendship might never recover. She didn't think there'd ever be one between Cade and Sam.

Mrs. Rodriguez stood and headed for the kettle. "Better?"

"Yes, I'm much better. I came in here to make tea. Oh! I forgot, I have a surprise for you." Sabrina knew there would be a connection between the motherless Bernice and the loving Mexican woman. "Come out to the saloon with me. There's someone you need to meet."

Wearing her standard scowl, Mrs. Rodriguez followed

Sabrina out to the saloon. Bernice ate peanuts at the bar, throwing them up in the air to catch them with her mouth. By the looks of the floor beneath the stool, her aim was awful. The remains of the shells were scattered on the usually pristine bar.

The scowl on the older woman's face deepened. "*¿Quién es esta niña?*"

"This is Bernice Wilkerson. She lost her pa to consumption last year and her ma when she was just a tot. Mr. Brody and I thought perhaps you and Antonio could open your home to her." She glanced at the girl, who had a shuttered, almost frightened look in her eyes. "Bernice, this is Consuela Rodriguez, the best cook in the entire county."

Bernice mumbled, "How do."

Mrs. Rodriguez walked around Bernice, her sharp gaze assessing the girl in the ill-fitting clothes and unkempt hair.

"*Con mucho gusto*, Bernice." She held out one wrinkled hand. "For you, I climb upstairs and pick a room, *hija.*"

Without hesitation, and surprising the heck out of Sabrina, the girl took Mrs. Rodriguez's proffered hand and they disappeared into the kitchen. Just like that Bernice had a new home and a family to love her.

Cade stood in the shadows of the hallway, keeping his breath shallow while his heart slammed against his ribs. Sabrina had told the old woman that she loved him. She *loved* him. Cade Brody had a woman who loved him. He never expected, *ever*, to have anyone love him. She'd confided it to someone else, but nevertheless, she loved *him*.

After Mrs. Rodriguez and the girl passed by, he let out a breath and felt light-headed. His ears rang, his eyes stung and his throat was tight. Is this what love was? It made him want to vomit and dance at the same time. He didn't know if he could take it much longer.

Cade needed to hear Sabrina say it to him, just once. A hunger built inside him that would only be appeased by the words *I love you* from the woman who owned his heart. It was more than need, more than desire or want, it was an absolute necessity to continue breathing.

He walked into the saloon and noticed Sabrina's red eyes and the handkerchief clutched in her hand. She'd been crying because of him. No one had ever cried for him either. Without another thought, he walked up and cupped her face.

"You deserve so much better than me." When his lips descended on hers, the ache in his throat eased, his eyes dried and his heart felt a thousand pounds lighter. Sabrina was the cure for what ailed him.

It started as a fierce kiss, but as her lips softened beneath his, he gentled his touch. Slow, sweet movements were followed by his tongue tickling her mouth open, like a soft invader sent to dance with hers. Their tongues rasped and slid against each other, as the heat built up between them.

"Ahem." Antonio cleared his throat behind them. "Your bedroom is not in my saloon, *amigos*."

Reluctantly, Cade broke the kiss and pulled back.

Her blue eyes sparkled with what could only be called joy. "I don't care what you think I deserve, I want you."

Cade couldn't speak so he only nodded. After tucking her under his arm, they turned to face a grinning Antonio.

"You sure you want to marry this man?" He winked at Sabrina.

"Yes." She spoke without hesitation, making Cade's heart beat faster, if it were possible.

"And you, you sure you want to marry Sabrina? She can be, ah, tough." Antonio's smile widened.

Cade thought of a million reasons why he should say no, but he couldn't. "Yeah, I'm sure."

"Good, then *felicitaciones*! You are married." Antonio rocked back on his heels, looking more than pleased with himself.

Cade didn't know what the hell he was talking about. "Are you a preacher?"

"Nope, but we only get one in here a couple times a year. When folks want to get married, they say so in front of a witness, that would be me, and then live together as husband and wife until the preacher comes to town to make it official." He glanced at Sabrina. "Ain't that right, *amiga*?"

She blushed and Cade knew what Antonio said was true. "Yes, that's right. I'd forgotten."

Cade's palms began to sweat as the realization swept through him. "You mean we're married. You're my wife and I'm your husband?"

Sabrina looked up at him, her heart shining brightly in her eyes. "For better or for worse."

After a moment's hesitation, he scooped her up in his arms and headed for the door.

"Where are you going?" Antonio called after them.

"To make love to my wife." Cade's comment drew a hearty laugh from his friend that followed him and Sabrina out into the cold.

"I need my coat," she murmured with a grin. "Although I like your enthusiasm."

"We won't need a coat to keep warm." His gaze locked with hers. "We'll make enough heat to last a lifetime."

She wrapped her arms around his neck. "I love you, Cade Brody."

That's when Cade fell completely in love with his new wife and knew his life had just made a radical course change. He'd never be the same again.

Chapter Ten

Sabrina's stomach jumped around with each step Cade took toward the store as the realization seeped through her that she loved him and now he was her husband. She'd never expected to marry again yet she easily jumped into his arms and wholeheartedly became his wife. The logistics of where they would live, what would happen to the store and all of that weren't important. What was important was that he accepted their inexorable mating.

"You surprised me," she whispered in his ear.

"I surprised myself." His dark gaze found hers. "Sometimes it's best not to think too hard and just do what your heart tells you to."

"I thought you said you didn't have a heart."

He pinched her fanny, making her squeal with indignation. "What did you do that for?"

"Because your ass is the only thing I can reach right now." He kissed her hard. "Except for those red lips of yours, of course."

"I'm disappointed." Ellen stood in the doorway to the

store, her arms folded across her chest and tears in her eyes.

"Put me down, Cade."

He complied immediately, setting her on her feet. She straightened her shirt and walked toward her sister, ready to face the consequences of her choice.

"Hello, Ellen."

Ellen's blue gaze darkened when she looked at Cade. "What did you do, Brina?"

"I followed my heart." Sabrina didn't want to be at odds with Ellen and hoped she wouldn't have to choose between her new husband and her sister.

"Your heart? It led you to a dark man with an even darker past. Don't you understand what you've done? Dark men can only bring destruction." Ellen's voice rose as she spoke.

"Let's go inside." Sabrina ushered her toward the door. "The entire town doesn't need to hear this conversation."

Ellen was as stiff as the icicles hanging from the roof, but she allowed Sabrina to lead her into the store. Once inside, Ellen closed the door on Cade, almost hitting him.

"He doesn't need to hear this." Her voice was firmer than Sabrina had ever heard.

Cade met Sabrina's gaze through the glass in the door. He nodded his understanding and moved out of sight. Already they were communicating silently, another sign they were connected, meant to be two halves of the same whole.

She turned to Ellen. "Now tell me what you're feeling."

Ellen threw her hands up in the air and starting walking around the store in circles. "You married him, didn't you? You knew how I felt about the darkness that surrounded him, yet you ignored all the warnings. I don't know what to do. You've set yourself up to fall into the pits of hell." Her blonde curls flew every which way as she gestured.

"Ellen, he isn't your husband and this isn't your life." There was just so far Sabrina would allow her sister to go.

"But you are my sister. What's going to happen to the store? You know I can't do the day-to-day things like you. The last two days have been so hard." Ellen's voice broke on the last word.

Sabrina stopped her mad pacing and enfolded her little sister in a hug. She trembled in her arms, reminding Sabrina that Ellen was not as strong as she'd like her to be.

"I'm sorry," she crooned. "I didn't mean to hurt you. Please understand that I love Cade."

"You love him?" Ellen pulled back, her tear-filled eyes wide.

"Yes, I do and I'm sure he loves me too. He hasn't had an easy life, which may be the darkness you see around him." It was important to Sabrina that her sister accept her new relationship with Cade.

"Sam told me he was a gunslinger." Ellen stepped away, wiping her eyes. "How could you love a man who

197

killed people for money?"

"Sam is jealous and you know it. He'd say anything to make Cade look bad to me and everyone else in Eustace." Sabrina closed her eyes. "I don't know what to say to convince you he's a good person, but I can only ask that you accept him as my husband."

"I don't know if I can," Ellen whispered.

Sabrina's heart sank. "You can't mean that."

"I don't want to lose you again, Brina." Ellen started crying anew, looking more like a five-year-old little girl than a woman in her twenties.

"You haven't lost me. I'm not going anywhere. I'll be here at the store with you, and perhaps this is your opportunity to come out of the shadows." She touched Ellen's scar. "You're a beautiful woman and have so much love to give. I wish you could see that."

"I'm ugly." Ellen shook her head. "I scare children."

"No, you're only scared of people staring at you. If you'd only realize it doesn't matter one whit what you look like, you could live like a normal person." Sabrina hadn't meant to snap like that, but it just came out.

Ellen reared back as if she'd been slapped. Her mouth opened and closed but all that came out was a gasp. Sabrina took her by the shoulders.

"You are such an amazing person, kind, sweet and smarter than all of us put together." Sabrina felt tears spring to her own eyes. "Please, Ellen, give life a chance, give me and Cade a chance, give yourself a chance. Please. Don't let Whit take your life too."

At the mention of her ex-fiancé, Ellen paled, but she stuck her chin in the air. "All right, I'll try," she whispered.

Sabrina's heart thumped with relief as a smile grew on her face. "Thank you, thank you, thank you."

As the sisters hugged, the door to the store opened and Jeremiah poked his head in.

"Has everybody gone loco? What in tarnation is going on here?" His floppy brown hair poked out from beneath a knit cap Sabrina recognized as Clara's. He had a crutch stuck under one arm.

"We're just talking, come on in." Sabrina opened the door wide and gestured for Jeremiah to step in. She looked out and saw Cade standing at the foot of the steps, coatless and stamping his feet against the cold.

With a nod from Ellen, Sabrina called her new husband. "Cade."

He whipped his head around, his dark gaze hidden beneath the ever-present black hat.

"Please come in." She held out her hand, and he walked up the stairs and into the rest of their lives.

They spent the rest of the day cleaning the store, stocking the shelves and getting to know each other. Ellen kept her distance from Cade, but she wasn't overtly hostile. Jeremiah chattered on about the ghost and how he'd seen her through Antonio's window. Cade laughed again, the second time he remembered the sensation tickling his belly, and it was all due to Sabrina.

That night would be their wedding night, when they consummated their marriage and completed the promise made between them. His jittery heart couldn't help but tremble at the thought. Who would have ever guessed a cold-hearted gunslinger could be nervous? Damn sure he didn't.

Jeremiah was like a puppy hobbling around behind Cade, wide-eyed at the man who pulled him from the jaws of death. The kid could talk until the sun went down and came up again. The only thing that saved his unworthy life was the heated gazes Sabrina kept aiming Cade's direction.

It kept his pants tight and his temper tamed. He felt like a different person those few hours they were in the store, almost normal. There might come a time when he'd look back and savor every second of it again and again, but for now he lived in every second, actually *lived* it.

He finally made his way over to Sabrina, intent on at least getting a kiss when the door to the store burst open. The bell went flying off the top, hitting Jeremiah in the head. Bernice stood in the doorway, her hair clean and in braids, looking like a young girl instead of a bear cub. However, she was breathing hard and her face was flushed.

"Brody, you got trouble." She slammed the door closed behind her, barely sparing the goggle-eyed Jeremiah a glance.

"I thought you were with Antonio and Mrs. Rodriguez." Cade frowned at the girl. "What do you mean

I've got trouble?"

"I was in the kitchen eating cornbread, dang they got good cornbread, and I saw a man come in the saloon. Sunday ain't a busy day Antonio says, so only a few folks were in there." She shot a glance at Ellen standing like a deer in hunter's sights. "Who's that?"

"That's my sister, Ellen." Sabrina made introductions as if they were at a Sunday social. "Ellen, this is Bernice Wilkerson. She's going to be living with the Rodriguezes."

To Cade's surprise, Ellen murmured a greeting without bolting for the stairs. Whatever Sabrina had said must've made a difference to the painfully shy blonde.

"How do." Bernice turned her gaze back to Cade. "This man come in, dirty and stinking like he'd had a week with cheap whiskey and a cheaper whore."

"Bernice!" Sabrina admonished.

"So's I kept my eye on him," Bernice continued as if Sabrina hadn't spoken. "He wore his guns low on his hips, a pair of them looking worn and well-used. Kinda reminded me of your guns."

"You got guns?" Jeremiah piped up.

"Shut up, kid." Cade's heart beat slow and dangerous, waiting for what Bernice was going to say before she even said it. "What happened?"

"He ate like a pig, sopping up the beans with his fingers. Reminded me of some of the nasty miners used to be around my pa. Anyways, he asks Antonio if he knows any strangers new to town." Bernice licked her lips while her gaze darted between Cade and Sabrina. "He said no, nobody in town was new. The stranger said he saw a wire asking about a dark-haired gunslinger in Eustace."

"Sweet Jesus." Sabrina grabbed Cade's arm while his stomach turned upside down.

"Who sent it?"

"Dunno. Probably that loud-mouthed fool that slapped Miss Sabrina." Bernice sneered. "I hope you kick his ass, Brody."

Cade held onto his temper by a thread. "The stranger, Bernice, what about the stranger?"

"Oh yeah, he drank some whiskey and eyeballed Antonio like he expect he'd been lied to."

"Did you get his name?" Cade's jaw tightened.

"I think it was Reynolds. I skedaddled outta there to come warn you there's another gunslinger in town and he's looking for you." Bernice's words fell like rocks in a pond, the ripples fanning out in the store, leaving dead silence behind them.

Sabrina's hand clenched his in a death grip. "Go upstairs."

Cade looked at her. "Have you lost your mind? I'm not hiding from Reynolds."

"You know him then?"

Memories washed over him, and a bad taste filled his mouth. "I know him."

"Then you can't possibly go out there. He'll recognize you." Sabrina tugged at his arm.

Ellen started to panic, her voice growing shrill.

Hell For Leather

"What's going on? Who is Reynolds and why is he looking for Mr. Brody?"

Bernice rolled her eyes. "Boy have you got a lot to learn."

Sabrina took control of the situation. "Bernice, go back to the saloon and tell Antonio to keep the man in whiskey, no matter what. I'll pay for it. Jeremiah, Marshal Black is likely still over at Clara's. Go get him and tell him we've got a situation."

Bernice waited for Cade to nod before she dashed out the door.

Jeremiah watched her go, a look of pure adulation on his face. "Ain't she amazing?"

"Get moving." Sabrina pushed him out the door. "Now."

He scampered away, hanging onto his hat with one hand while he carefully maneuvered down the snowy steps toward Clara's small house. Cade started after him, determined to get rid of Reynolds before he did harm to the folks he'd come to know and appreciate, some of them even love. No fucking way he'd let that happen.

Sabrina blocked his way, her eyes blazing fire. "Go upstairs."

"I am not hiding behind a woman's skirts. You are *not* going to be hurt because of me."

She held up her hand as if to stop him. "And I will not allow my husband to die on our wedding day because he's a stubborn ass."

Cade would've smiled if it had been any other moment in time, but he could feel his happiness slipping through his fingers by the second. "Come in here with me."

He pulled her into her office, the curtain the only barrier against the big ears listening in the store. "You will *not* put yourself in danger for me." Cade's head pounded with the need to protect her.

"Why not? You are my husband now and I don't want to lose you." She put her hands on her hips. "You can't stop me."

"Just listen." His throat tightened at what he was about to reveal, but he had to stop her in any way he could. "I am not a good person, hell, I'm hardly a person. Let me tell you what your husband has done in his lifetime, then you can decide if he's worth saving."

"Stop it." She pushed at his chest, anger stamped on her face. "I won't listen to you beat yourself up."

"Oh yes you will." He pinched the bridge of his nose. "Please."

"Whatever you have to say won't change my mind." She threw her hands up in the air. "But obviously you won't let me go until you speak your peace, so get on with it."

She knew as well as he did that Reynolds could saunter over to the store at any moment. Eustace wasn't that big—it only took about ten minutes to search every building in town.

"I was born in a bordello in New Orleans called Kincaid's. My mother was an opium addict who let men do whatever they wanted to her for money. She barely tolerated the sight of me so the other *ladies* there raised me." He leaned against the desk as buried memories rose from their graves, filling him with the self-hate he'd come to know. "She died when I was four and the madam of the house only let me stay there if I started, ah, helping the ladies." Cade swallowed hard, the tightness in his throat only getting worse.

"Help them how?" Sabrina's voice was barely above a whisper.

"While their customers were busy fucking, I'd steal whatever they had in their pockets. The madam had a little door in the corner with tunnels between the rooms. I learned a lot by watching what was going on, more than any boy should know. I crawled through the rat shit and dirt for another six or seven years, until I got too big to fit. Then she had another job for me." Cade's hands curled into fists and he hardly resisted the urge to slam them into Sabrina's desk. "Some of the clients wanted young boys instead of young girls."

He let that sink in and when it did, Sabrina gasped. This was the moment she'd renounce him as her husband and let him go face Reynolds alone. He braced himself for the revulsion and the rejection. Instead, her hands flattened against his back.

"Oh God, Cade, I'm so sorry." Her voice was thick with tears.

So was his.

"I stayed until I was thirteen and big enough to do

some damage to the rougher clients. The madam threw me out and I had nothing but the clothes on my back and a mean streak a mile wide." He laughed, a scraping sound that made her hands twitch on his shirt. "I found an old man named Reynolds who taught me what he knew about guns, for a price. I stole for him too, everything and anything. One night he tried"—he swallowed the bile that rose up his throat—"to force me to lay under him so I killed him with his own gun."

Sabrina pressed her face into his back now, openly weeping, *for him.* Cade couldn't stop now if a lightning bolt hit the building.

"I was fast, really fast with the pistols, and I practiced until I was unstoppable. Soon I was building a reputation and when folks asked me my name, I had to invent one. You see, the only name I ever had was 'boy' or 'kid'. My mother never bothered to give me a name. Some of the ladies in the bordello used to call me Cade since I was born at Kincaid's, and as a gunslinger, there was only one name I could use. I'm Kincaid." He straightened and turned around, grabbing her wrists. Sabrina's tear-stained face wasn't repulsed or even disgusted. She looked as if she was in pain, as if his story were hers.

"I've killed one hundred and seven men, Sabrina. Some of them for money, others who thought they were better than me." Tears stung his eyes. He had to convince her he wasn't worth her life. "I'm a piece of shit born from a hellhole I wouldn't even want to pass on the street. Don't cry for me and you sure as hell shouldn't die for me."

She shook her head. "Love doesn't care where you came from or what you've done. Love only knows what's in your heart." Wiggling her wrist free from his grasp, she flattened her palm against his chest, his stupid heart beating a loud tattoo beneath it. "In here, you are the man I love, the man I would give my life for. You cannot stop me, and your story only makes me love you more."

Cade couldn't believe Sabrina. How could she possibly still love him?

"Didn't you hear what I said? I haven't done anything in my life except cause misery and pain." He trembled from head to toe. "Sabrina, you've got to let me go."

"Never." She stepped away and wiped her eyes with her sleeve. "I don't care what dark hole you think you crawled out of, but you're in my light now. I am going to save your life, Cade Brody, or whatever your name is, and then we'll start the rest of our lives together. I will not let you die. *Stay here.*" Her fierceness made his throat close up with what could only be love.

"Jesus, Sabrina, what the hell am I supposed to do?" He'd never had a wife or anyone who cared what happened to him. And he sure as hell never expected her to try to protect him, especially when she knew his every dirty secret.

"You're supposed to let me do what I can to save your life." She grabbed her coat from the hook next to the desk and her rifle from the wall above. "For God's sake, go upstairs and wait." She cupped his face and kissed him softly. "I love you."

Sabrina disappeared through the curtain, leaving a wake of confusion in his head and carrying his heart with her.

The afternoon air had grown colder with the sun setting behind her. Sabrina ran like the hounds of hell were chasing her, knowing she'd likely only have one chance to save Cade and she was taking it. Her heart ached for the boy who'd had nothing but misery his entire life, yet still had the capacity to care, to love. There was no way he'd die that day—Sabrina would save him come hell or high water. Cade deserved a chance at happiness.

She looked for Jeremiah and Marshal Black, but they were nowhere to be seen on the street. However, Sam intercepted her on the way to the Last Gate.

"Where are you going?" He fell into stride next to her. "And why are you carrying that rifle?"

"I'm saving my husband's life. That gunslinger in there is after Cade because of you." She pointed an accusing finger at him. "You sent wires around, didn't you?"

Sam had the audacity to look proud of it. "I was protecting me and mine."

"Sam, I am not yours and I don't need protecting. He's a good man, one who's done nothing but help the folks in Eustace, and you threw it back in his face." She pushed Sam away. "I can't talk to you right now without wanting to shoot you myself. Now go back to the mill and think about what you've done."

"I didn't do anything."

"You didn't? You put every person in this town in danger by bringing an armed man gunning for Cade in its midst by sending out those damn telegrams. Anyone could be hurt, including Melissa." She held up the rifle. "These weapons don't care who gets killed, and neither does that man in there. I, on the other hand, care a great deal about who gets killed, namely no one."

"Sabrina, I—"

"Stop it, Sam. I don't want to hear it anymore." She lengthened her strides, leaving Sam to wallow in his own self-pity. There wasn't time for it.

When she got to the saloon, she pressed her ear against the door and strained to hear what was going on. All she could hear were low murmurs coming from inside, which told her nothing. Sabrina was scared, more scared than she'd ever been in her life, but she wouldn't stop now. Her throat felt as dry as her mouth and her heart pounded madly.

Sabrina pushed the door open and stepped in.

Cade pulled the curtain aside and peered out the window. She'd been gone for five minutes and already he couldn't stand one more second of waiting.

"She loves you." Bernice had impeccable timing.

"Yes, I know, brat. Go away." His hand tightened on the lace until he heard a ripping sound.

"She told you t'stay here, but you're not gonna listen,

are you?" Bernice's gaze was sharper than any thirteen-year-old ought to have.

"Shut up, Bernice." He let the curtain drop and turned back to the store. Ellen stared at him from behind the counter, and for a change her hair was pulled back into a braid, exposing her entire face.

He didn't know what had happened between Sabrina and her sister, but something must have. Ellen had hidden in the shadows every time he'd seen her, and now she was standing in the full light of the afternoon sun, showing the world her scar. Cade walked toward her, and to her credit, she visibly tightened but didn't move.

"Sabrina does whatever she wants to do, no matter what anyone says otherwise." Ellen's voice was firmer and more in control too. "If you want a true marriage, then you've got to be a true partner."

The last thing he expected was to hear Ellen favoring their marriage and giving advice on how to stay married. His head and his heart finally knew what he had to do.

"I have a gun."

That stopped him in his tracks. He stared hard at Ellen. "You do?"

"It was my father's. I never took to the rifles like Sabrina did, but my papa wanted to make sure I could protect myself. I never carried it, stupid decision, and when fate came calling, I ended up looking like this." She gestured to the scar. "I won't ever make that mistake again."

Cade held out his hand. "Where is it?"

She pulled a Colt .45 out from beneath the counter, along with a dozen bullets. "It's not loaded, but it's clean." Ellen pushed it toward him. "Do you love her?"

A moment passed, then two while Cade wrestled with himself. "Yeah, I do."

"Then don't let anything happen to her, and for God's sake, don't ever let her go."

Cade took Ellen's hand and planted a hard kiss on the back. "I won't. Thank you, my new sister."

Bernice stood by the open door. "You'd better move your ass, Brody."

Cade ran toward the door. "Shut up, Bernice."

Sabrina stepped into the saloon with the rifle hidden in the folds of her skirt, her heart residing somewhere near her throat. Antonio stood behind the bar, his expression set in stone. When he spotted her, surprise led to annoyance.

"You shouldn't be here." He pulled her into the hallway and his gaze dropped to the rifle in her hand. "Sabrina, what the hell are you doing?"

"Protecting my town and the people I love." She glanced around the saloon, noting the large man sitting in the shadows at a table. "Where's Johnathan Black?"

"Not here."

Sabrina knew she couldn't take on the gunslinger alone. "We need him here."

"We need an army." Antonio's attempt at humor fell

flat.

Sabrina had an idea. "Tell him to leave."

"What?" Antonio looked at her as if she'd lost her mind.

"We can't get rid of him if his ass is stuck to that chair. Now tell him to leave." She peeked around the corner at the stranger.

"Fine." Antonio went back into the saloon and stepped toward the stranger in the corner. "*Señor*, it's siesta time, so we're closing."

"Siesta?" The man's gravelly voice sent shivers up Sabrina's spine. "I'm thinking you just want to fuck your *puta* in there."

To his credit, Antonio only blinked. "Every day, *señor*. We open up again after supper."

"I don't take no siesta like you lazy Mexicans. Just leave the bottle." He chuckled at his own joke. Sabrina had never felt the urge to shoot someone, but this man might change her mind for the second time in one day.

Antonio's knuckles cracked as his hands fisted. Sabrina thought violence was about to erupt when Mrs. Rodriguez appeared from the kitchen. She threw her arms in the air and started yelling in Spanish. After she pushed Sabrina toward the door, she yelled at Antonio.

"*¡Hijo malo! Es la hora de tomar una siesta, estúpido.*" She turned her sharp gaze on Reynolds. "*Salga del edificio, ahora.*"

When he stood, she didn't flinch an inch against the

man's great height.

"*Ahora.*" She pointed outside.

To Sabrina's surprise, the stranger threw back the whiskey in the glass in front of him and started to leave.

"Fine then, just get this old bitch away from me." He hitched up his gun belt and belched. "I don't feel like killing her."

Antonio apologized to his mother. "*Lo siento, Mamá.*" He shrugged at Reynolds. "My mother owns the saloon, *señor*, so I do what she says."

Reynolds snorted as he walked toward the door. "What a pussy."

Sabrina ducked outside and stood to the left of the building, waiting for the man to come out who wanted to kill her husband. Her hand tightened on the rifle grip even as the door opened.

To her surprise, Sam appeared with a rifle in hand, beside Clara toting a shotgun. Jeremiah was using a shovel as a crutch, his expression fierce. Behind them came Hiram, Frenchie and Bernice, all carrying picks and shovels.

Reynolds came outside and frowned at the crowd of folks walking toward him. "What the hell is this?"

Sabrina pulled the rifle up and pointed it at the gunslinger. "We want you to leave town, mister. We don't take to strangers threatening us." She pulled the hammer back, her sweaty palms gripping the handle as tightly as she could.

"I ain't leaving until I find Kincaid. I know he's here." Reynolds's gaze raked her up and down, then focused on the rifle. "You ready to kill me, you fat cow?"

She held onto her temper by a thread. "Don't doubt it. I protect my own." The nervousness disappeared as righteous anger coursed through her. "Get out of Eustace."

Reynolds laughed and caressed the grips of his guns. "I like you. You got spunk. Too bad I might have to kill you too. Now where's Kincaid?"

Sabrina walked toward him, her friends behind her ready to do battle for the man who told her ten minutes ago he wasn't even a person. He might not believe it yet, but Cade was more than a person, he was part of their family. And this family protected its own.

"You heard the lady, get out of town." Sam cocked his rifle and aimed it at Reynolds. "We don't want your kind here."

"My kind? Ha, from what I heard Kincaid's only been living here a couple of months. He's worse than I am. The man is a killing machine." Reynolds stepped out into the street.

Sabrina didn't know what would happen if Reynolds refused to leave. He was a trained killer and she and her friends just ordinary folks. They'd need more than a couple rifles and shovels to make him go.

"The marshal is on the way. He's going to make sure you leave town." Sabrina settled the rifle on her shoulder and got Reynolds in her sights. "You might want to leave before he gets here."

Reynolds narrowed his gaze. "Are you threatening me?"

"Absolutely." Sabrina widened her stance as Eric had taught her to, ready to take the brunt of the shot. It was as if her first husband helped her protect her second, a warm feeling that filled her with strength. "Now leave."

She heard a few more guns cock as she focused entirely on Reynolds. The pity was he wasn't a hideous monster as she'd expected. He was even handsome, although the sneer on his face ruined the effect. He could have been any man she met on any day, but he was a gunslinger out to murder her husband.

"I don't want to kill you, but I will." Reynolds turned toward her, widening his stance, hands hovering over his pistols. "You ready to dance with me?"

"She's not who you want." Cade's voice came from behind Sabrina.

"Dammit, Cade. Why don't you listen to me?" She didn't dare take her gaze off Reynolds, although she wanted to smack Cade. If he got himself killed, she'd follow him just to kick his ass for being so stubborn and stupid.

"Kincaid." Reynolds sounded like a man who'd found a gold mine. "It's about time. I was beginning to think you were going to hide behind a woman's skirts."

"I ain't hiding from nothing." Cade stepped up beside her. "I'm here now so you can take your sights off her."

Reynolds's eyebrows rose. "So she your woman? A

good fuck then? I'll find out later after I dance on your rotting corpse."

Sabrina growled. "You son of a bitch."

Cade touched her arm. "Stand down, Brina. This is one thing I do really good."

"Let's do this, Kincaid. I've been waiting twenty years to spill your blood, ever since you killed my pa." Reynolds's hands settled on the guns.

"I did the world a favor killing your pa. He spent his life stealing from people and fucking little bo—"

The next five seconds were a blur of smoke and guns, each blast echoing through her ears. Sabrina pulled the trigger, but she didn't know where her bullet ended up and hoped it didn't hurt anyone but the gunslinger trying to kill her husband. When the smoke cleared, both Cade and Reynolds lay on the ground.

Sabrina threw the rifle and dropped to her knees. "You stupid fool! Why didn't you listen to me? I was trying to save you, don't you understand? I can't lose you so soon after I found you." She frantically searched his body for blood, a wound, anything, but couldn't find a thing. "Cade, what happened?" Sobs burst from her throat.

"Jesus, woman, can't you handle a rifle?" Cade groaned and put a hand on his forehead. "You knocked me on my ass with your elbow after the recoil."

She threw herself on top of him, kissing his face while laughing, crying and shouting. He was alive!

"You scared me." She wiped her eyes and looked down into the dark depths of her husband's eyes. "Why didn't you stay at the store?"

"I forgot to tell you something."

Sabrina waited for what he would say, knowing what it was before he said it. "So tell me already and I'll let you up. That snow must be cold."

He touched her cheek with trembling fingers. "I love you."

"I love you too." Her heart soared with joy and relief as they both stood, brushing the snow from their clothes.

"Well, this'un is dead for sure." Frenchie stood over Reynolds's body. "Got hit twice, once in the eye and t'other in the heart. Fancy shooting for a man who don't own a gun." The old miner eyed the pistol on the ground.

"That's my pa's gun, Frenchie. Ellen must have given it to him." She hooked her arm through his. "After all, he's family."

Clara poked the gunslinger with her small foot. "Well, let's get a hole dug before the sun sets so we can get rid of this trash."

Marshal Black chose to appear at that moment, his sharp gaze missing nothing. "It appears a man tried to assault Mrs. Brody and her husband protected her."

Sabrina realized right then the marshal knew exactly who Cade was, or used to be anyway. If Johnathan had been there he would have had to break up the gunfight, perhaps even arrest Reynolds. However, the marshal let it all happen, to let the past be buried with the man who tried to resurrect another.

"It's a good thing you folks were around to help out. Mr. Brody, I'm glad you're all right."

Cade glanced at the folks gathered around him. "I can't say thank you enough to everyone for trying to protect me. I ain't never really had a family before now."

"Well you've got one now whether or not you want one." Antonio laughed, his mother clutching Bernice to her like a mother hen.

"Welcome to Eustace, Mr. Brody." Clara inclined her head. "You take care of our Sabrina now."

"I intend to." He looked into Sabrina's eyes. "I can't imagine ever doing anything else."

Sam walked up and stuck out his hand. "I lost my head, Brody, and for that I apologize to both of you. Sabrina, I know you're mad at me, but maybe one day we can be friends again." He tipped his hat and walked back to the mill with Hiram.

Marshal Black stepped up to Cade and spoke quietly. "We have a mutual friend, don't you know. Tyler Calhoun sends his regards." He shook Cade's hand too. "Miss Clara, I'd be happy to assist you in picking a likely grave spot." He offered her his arm and the four-foot woman walked off with the six-foot lawman toward the cemetery.

"Well, hell, I didn't expect that, any of it." Cade's throat worked as he apparently tried to clear out whatever had affected him.

"Who's Tyler Calhoun?" Sabrina picked up the rifle and pistol.

Cade didn't offer to touch the weapons and for that

she was grateful. He might pick up a gun to save her life, but his actions spoke volumes about his distaste for it. The gunslinger Kincaid was truly dead.

"Have I ever told you about Brett Malloy?" He walked beside her as they headed back to the store.

"No, or maybe. I'm not sure." She had a feeling the story was important.

"I met him back in the spring in Cheyenne, Wyoming. I'd been hired to kill his brother's woman."

Sabrina sucked in a breath. Someone would hire a gunslinger to kill a woman?

"Don't worry, honey, I didn't do it. Somehow, me and Brett, well, we understood each other. He became the first friend I ever had, gave me a chance to learn on his ranch, even let me meet his family." He looked up into the sky. "My reputation nearly got him killed so I left and came here."

"Sounds like it was hard for you to leave, but I'm glad you did otherwise I wouldn't have met you." She kissed his neck. "That still doesn't answer the question, who's Tyler Calhoun?"

Cade laughed. "Brett's brother-in-law. He's an ex-bounty hunter who seems to know every lawman in the west. I thought I left them behind, but they're still with me." His eyes were shiny in the fading sunlight. "I never knew what family was."

Sabrina hugged him close. "Well now you do. Everyone deserves folks who love them and care for them. You, my dear husband, have both."

As Cade embraced her tightly in the orange rays of the sunset, she felt him tremble. A quiet hiccup in his chest told her that even a man who thinks he's not a person can love and be loved, so she let him cry, safe in her arms.

Cade was nervous, an unfamiliar and unsettling emotion. Darkness has settled its blanket on the cold night beyond the windows, and he waited for his wife. She insisted on freshening up in the room next to hers and made him wait by her bed, *their* bed. His palms felt like they'd been dipped in cold water and damned if his hands weren't shaking.

What the hell was wrong with him? Everything was perfect in his life, he had a wife who loved him, a town that accepted him and his identity was now firmly Cade Brody. There was no reason to be nervous, but he was.

He'd shucked his shirt and trousers, but left his drawers on for some reason. It wasn't as if she hadn't seen him naked before. As he picked up his shirt to wipe the sweat off his hands, the bedroom door opened. He looked up to find the woman of his dreams walking toward him.

"Holy shit."

Sabrina must have had a hidden treasure of fancy underthings in the store. She wore a diaphanous blue nightgown that matched her eyes. Through the sheer fabric, he saw the outline of her nipples and the triangle of her pussy. The door closed behind her and he jumped.

"Do you like it?" She walked around in a circle, the fabric fanning out like a wave around her.

"Jesus, if I like it anymore, I'm going to need new drawers." He swallowed with difficulty, at her mercy without even a touch.

Sabrina laughed. That husky sound went straight to his dick, which was already standing straight and tall. She glided toward the bed, a welcoming smile on her face until she got close enough to see his chest, and then she frowned.

Without asking any questions, she put her warm palms on his skin. "You've had so much pain in your life. I want to take it all away."

When her lips touched the first scar, a shudder wracked his body. Each kiss reinforced the love they shared, the connection between them growing deeper and stronger. He could have stopped her, but he didn't. The sweet warmth of her kisses filled him with hope and healing.

"God, I love you." The words were torn from the depths of his wounded soul.

She straightened and kissed his lips. "Make love to me, husband."

Cade didn't think he could have asked for a more perfect moment. He peeled the gown from her shoulders, enjoying the play of the fabric as it caught on her nipples. They popped free, rock-hard raspberry peaks begging for his touch.

He dropped to his knees and cupped the orbs, his

thumbs rubbing back and forth. She gasped and clenched his shoulders. As his mouth closed around the left one, his hand continued to pleasure the other. He nibbled, licked and sucked her over and over, as she trembled beneath his touch.

"Cade, I...can't," she gasped out. "Please."

He pulled the gown completely down and then scooped her up in his arms, eager to make her his wife in truth. After he laid her on the white coverlet, she spread her legs, giving him a glimpse of the pink flesh glistening with her arousal.

Cade yanked off his drawers and climbed onto the bed.

She opened her arms, pulling him atop her. "Please don't make me wait any longer."

"It might not be long, period," he choked out. "I've never been so hard in my life."

Sabrina laughed. "Ah, but we have all night, my love." She ran her hands down his back, leaving shivers behind.

He settled above her, poised at her entrance, and looked into her beautiful blue eyes. In their depths, he saw everything he could ever wish for, dream of or want. *She* was everything.

As he slid into her welcoming warmth, inch by inch, he reveled in the fact that she was his and he was hers. Once he was fully sheathed within her, he stopped to catch his breath, almost overwhelmed with the need to reach his peak already.

She rocked against him, drawing him in a tiny bit

further. "Oh God, Cade, please."

He couldn't wait a second longer either. Sabrina pulled her knees back, opening herself up to him fully. Her heat surrounded him as he thrust in and out, basking in the white light of their love.

"Cade, I am nearly there." Her voice was husky with passion.

"Now, Brina, now." He rode the wave of ecstasy that washed over him, finally feeling complete in her arms.

"Cade!" Sabrina cried his name into his ear, a whisper that resonated in his heart.

"My wife." Cade felt the truth of the words deep inside him—he'd finally found where he belonged.

About the Author

You can't say cowboys without thinking of Beth Williamson. She likes 'em hard, tall and packing. Read her work and discover for yourself how hot and dangerous a cowboy can be.

Beth lives in North Carolina, with her husband and two sons. Born and raised in New York, she holds a B.F.A. in writing from New York University. She spends her days as a technical writer, and her nights immersed in writing hot romances for her readers.

To learn more about Beth Williamson, please visit www.bethwilliamson.com. Sign up for Beth's monthly newsletter, Sexy Spurs:

www.janusportal.com/lists/?p=subscribe&id=3.

When a man sets out to tame a strong-willed woman,
he'd best hang on to his hat.

Taming Eliza Jane
© 2007 Shannon Stacey

Will Martinson, the town doctor, already has a heap of troubles on his plate, what with a pregnant whore, an ailing friend and a sheriff with a bad habit of shooting people. The last thing he needs is a strong hankering for a woman who thinks it's her duty to turn a man's life upside-down.

Eliza Jane Carter is a woman on a mission. She's going to improve the lives of the women in Gardiner, Texas before moving on to the next town. But when her finances take a turn for the worse and her chaperone heads for the hills, Eliza Jane is stranded in a town full of riled up menfolk, a gun-happy sheriff and one handsome doctor who makes her question everything she ever believed about the love between a man and a woman.

Available now in ebook and print from Samhain Publishing.

Enjoy the following excerpt from Taming Eliza Jane...

Women, in general, were more of a pain in the ass than a lumpy saddle. And whores, in particular, could drive a sober man to go looking for the bottom of a bottle.

The one between whose thighs Will Martinson currently knelt—a particular favorite of his by the name of Sadie—giggled again, causing her ample breasts to shake. It was more of a distraction than any man could withstand. But Sadie liked baring them, even though he'd told her time and time again he had no need to see them.

"It ain't supposed to tickle, Sadie."

"I ain't laughin' at no tickle. Was laughin' at your face—so serious and businesslike."

Will pushed to his feet and flipped Sadie's skirt down over her splayed thighs. "When were your last courses?"

The amusement drained from the pretty whore's face. "Do I gotta baby in me, Doc?"

Will sighed and closed up his bag. His monthly health checks at the Chicken Coop were usually uneventful. Miss Adele took good care of her girls, and taught them to care for themselves. But he was especially fond of Sadie—a dirt-poor Southern farm girl who'd probably never make it to California no matter how much time she spent on her back—and her expression damn near broke his heart.

"I think you do, Sadie." And not the first inkling of which of her numerous customers may have fathered it.

Not that it mattered. A whore's bastard was a child only the mother would love.

"How long can I work?"

His fingers tightened on the straps of his medical bag. "You should get on the next stage and go home, sweetheart. I'll pay your passage if you don't have enough money tucked away. Tell your folks you had a husband but he got killed."

A look of revulsion passed over her face. He saw that look a lot if he mentioned *home* during his visits to the Coop. What horrors these girls had been born into that made it preferable to spread their legs for an endless stream of strange men, he couldn't even begin to guess.

"I asked you," Sadie insisted, some of the sweetness gone from her voice, "how long can I work?"

Looking down into her pretty hazel eyes, framed by a mass of golden curls, he almost offered to marry her. She'd make a right sweet wife and she could be a proper mother to her baby. And if the people of Gardiner took issue with their doctor marrying a whore, why they could deliver their own babies and set their own goddamn broken bones.

He took a deep breath and settled his hat on his head. But, *hellfire,* he couldn't save them all.

"I guess until the men ain't willing to pay for you anymore," he replied in a voice heavy with regret.

Will walked out of the Chicken Coop with an aching heart and a gut churning with frustration. The last person he expected to see waiting for him was the sheriff, who usually gave the only whorehouse in town a wide berth.

Adam Caldwell was damn near the best friend Will had ever had, but he could be as much a pain in the ass as the whores at times. He wasn't sure he had the patience for him right now.

The sheriff fell into step beside him on the plank sidewalk. Will knew they made a noticeable pair. Adam was dark and forbidding. Over six feet of sun-darkened muscle, black shirt and a black hat covering long black hair, with unforgiving eyes almost as dark. They all figured there was some Indian in him somewhere, but no man had yet had the balls to ask him outright.

Will himself was as tall, but he was leaner, with an open, friendly air about him. White shirt with cuffs rolled to the elbows tucked into denim pants. His battered, brown Stetson covered sandy hair he kept trimmed off his ears and neck. And the ladies sure did tend to go on about his blue eyes.

The only other things they had in common were the tin stars—Will liked to pin his on his doctoring kit—and the holsters low on their hips. Will Martinson had sworn to preserve life, but he was also the only man Adam trusted to back him up. The sheriff's reputation went a long way toward keeping the peace, but when there was need for a deputy, Will just told himself there was more than one way to preserve a life.

"Trouble?" Adam finally asked when Will didn't talk just to fill the silence as he was wont to do.

"Sadie's with child."

Adam shrugged. "Can't help those who don't wanna be helped, Doc."

Hell, he knew that. But he wasn't in the mood to hear it just yet. "Heard at the Coop some woman got off the stage and stayed off."

It was a rare event for a woman to stay in town, unless her intention was a room at the Chicken Coop. Word of her had spread through Gardiner like wildfire.

"Yup. Ain't good."

Will waited for his friend to go on with a growing sense of aggravation. *Hellfire*, he'd had easier conversations with mules. "Why ain't it good? She somebody you've heard of?"

"Yup. Eliza Jane Carter. Likes to ride into town, get the women all riled up about demanding their rights and shit, then she skedaddles."

"She stayin' a while?"

"Looks like."

Will knew his friend was mulling over the woman's unwelcome presence in his town and her potential for troublemaking, but all he could think about was how the woman could maybe talk some sense into Sadie. Tell her there were better ways for her and her child to make it in the world.

Adam sighed and pushed his hat back on his head. "If the women gettin' riled up gets the men riled up, we could have us some trouble."

Damnation. He didn't need spectacles to see where

Adam was heading with this. "Dammit, Adam, I'm a doctor, not a nanny."

"Better job for you than me. I ain't so good with diplomacy."

"Diplomacy? You? Shit, they say you shot a man for calling your horse ugly."

The sheriff shrugged. "He lived. And my horse ain't ugly."

Fact was, Sheriff Caldwell's gelding was the ugliest son of a bitch to ever stand on four legs. A sane man would have shot the creature just to save his own eyesight. But that horse had speed and stamina the likes of which Will had never seen, and he would run until his heart exploded for Adam. He was loyal in a way Will hadn't come across even in a good dog, and certainly never in another person. Didn't change the fact the beast was damn ugly, though. Folks had just gotten real quiet about it.

"I ain't asking you to marry the woman, Doc. Just keep an eye on her." When Will hesitated, Adam shrugged again. Hell, he hated that—made Will want to shove the sheriff's head so far down his neck he could never shrug his shoulders again. "I'd hate for her to cause trouble. Seems a mighty shame to shoot a woman."

Will laughed at the blatant attempt at blackmail, some of the tension easing from his body. "Even you wouldn't shoot a woman, you ornery son of a bitch."

He looked up in time to see a damn fine looking woman step out of the hotel. She was tall and thin, but not so thin she didn't have rounded breasts and hips that like to make a man's mouth water. "Is that her?"

"Must be."

Will smiled and pushed his own hat back a little further on his head. "It *would* be a damn shame to have to shoot her."

"Yup."

She liked to get women all riled up about their rights, did she? "Could be she starts causing too much trouble I'll have to put her over my knee and spank some sense into her."

And damned if he didn't get so riled up himself he had to walk down the sidewalk with his bag held in front of his crotch like a schoolboy.

GREAT cheap fun

Discover eBooks!

THE FASTEST WAY TO GET THE HOTTEST NAMES

Get your favorite authors on your favorite reader, long before they're out in print! Ebooks from Samhain go wherever you go, and work with whatever you carry—Palm, PDF, Mobi, and more.

Samhain Publishing LTD

WWW.SAMHAINPUBLISHING.COM

Printed in the United Kingdom by
Lightning Source UK Ltd., Milton Keynes
138433UK00001B/163/P

9 781605 041650